"What Do You Want of Me?"

Her voice was husky as she spoke.

The grip on her wrist tightened, then shifted as Quinn stood. Before he answered, he pulled her to him, taking the sweep of her red-gold hair in his hand and holding her head immobile. His darkened eyes caressed her face, resting on her slightly parted lips as though anticipating the coming moment when he would capture them with his own.

"What do I want of you . . . ?" His voice was thoughtful. "Everything. Everything you have to give, Cara. Witch . . . my witch. . . . Your green eyes bewitch me and I want you."

CONSTANCE CONRAD

is a woman of many talents. Potter, painter, writer, and avid reader, she likes to draw on her own life experiences for the background material of her books. She used time spent at the Fashion Institute of Technology in New York as the inspiration for this, her first Silhouette Desire.

Dear Reader:

SILHOUETTE DESIRE is an exciting new line of contemporary romances from Silhouette Books. During the past year, many Silhouette readers have written in telling us what other types of stories they'd like to read from Silhouette, and we've kept these comments and suggestions in mind in developing SILHOUETTE DESIRE.

DESIREs feature all of the elements you like to see in a romance, plus a more sensual, provocative story. So if you want to experience all the excitement, passion and joy of falling in love, then SILHOUETTE DESIRE is for you.

I hope you enjoy this book and all the wonderful stories to come from SILHOUETTE DESIRE. I'd appreciate any thoughts you'd like to share with us on new SILHOUETTE DESIRE, and I invite you to write to us at the address below:

Karen Solem
Editor-in-Chief
Silhouette Books
P.O. Box 769
New York, N.Y. 10019

CONSTANCE CONRAD
On Wings Of Night

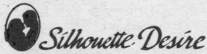

Silhouette Desire

Published by Silhouette Books New York

America's Publisher of Contemporary Romance

SILHOUETTE BOOKS, a Simon & Schuster Division of
GULF & WESTERN CORPORATION
1230 Avenue of the Americas, New York, N.Y. 10020

ISBN: 0-671-45381-5

First Silhouette Books printing November, 1982

10 9 8 7 6 5 4 3 2 1

America's Publisher of Contemporary Romance

Printed in the U.S.A.

On Wings
Of Night

1

The young woman huddled deeper into the folds of the long black velvet cape which she had wrapped tightly around herself. She sat motionless in the corner, ignoring the few passengers that were riding the early morning Lexington Avenue Subway. Her forehead wrinkled as she tried to understand how she could have found herself at five A.M. this morning in the bed of a man who was a total stranger to her.

It had all started at the Halloween celebration the preceding night; aside from the Beaux Arts Ball it was the most important social function sponsored by the Art Institute. She could remember Jenny telling her about the well-known guests that would be there.

"You have to go, Cara. You never know when you'll meet someone who might be able to help you once you're out in the business world trying to earn a living. Besides, maybe you'll find an interesting man looking for someone special like you." The lively little blonde pinned the layered skirt to the tight bodice of the witch's costume she was making for Cara, accenting her words with a vigorous push on each pin. "This is going to look gorgeous when I'm finished. With your white skin and red hair, you'll be a knockout. I'll never know why I agreed to room with you. I can't begin to compete with your looks."

"Come on, Jen . . ." Cara protested with a laugh. "You've got more men running after you than I can count on my fingers and toes! What more do you want?"

"I want you to have some fun!" Jenny stood up and moved away from Cara to take a long look at the elegantly seductive witch she had created. "You've been widowed for almost two years and you haven't had a proper date yet. It's just not right . . . you should be out having a ball, not moping around with nothing to do but class projects. For heaven's sake, you're only twenty-eight, not seventy-eight . . . and even if you were that old, you still ought to go out!"

"I do . . . I date Robert. It's just not easy to meet someone old enough for me. Most of the students are under twenty-one, and I'm not up to robbing the cradle yet." Carefully Cara began to remove the pinned-together costume. "Anyway, I didn't go back to school for the social life—I came for a degree."

"Oh, Robert." From the tone of her voice it was clear that she didn't approve of the design professor who had hired Cara as his part-time assistant. "He's about as exciting as a . . . a . . . toothpick! Don't you see that he's using you? He may be a good professor, but he's not creative. If you weren't such a talented interior designer, he'd have a hard time satisfying his finicky clients. And you'd still get your degree!"

"Oh, come on, Jenny, he's not as bad as all that." The red-haired girl handed the gossamer dress to her friend. "I'm learning a lot about the business end of decorating from him. He never tries anything with me. He knows I'm just not ready for any serious commitment."

"I'm not telling you to fall into bed with the first guy who comes along, dummy, but at least try dating someone who has a little more on the ball than good old Robert."

The roommates had continued to bicker back and forth over Cara's social life. Jenny finally won and Cara agreed to "loosen up" at the Halloween party. "And you promise to dance with whomever I introduce you to . . . even if you don't want to at first?"

"What am I letting myself in for?" Cara had wailed. "You'll probably set me up with a Don Juan. I'll never forgive you, Jenny, if you embarrass me," she had threatened.

Cara then recalled the way the previous evening had begun. Jenny and Rick, her off-again-on-again boy friend, had originally intended to accompany Cara to the dance but without Jenny's knowledge, Rick had accepted a dinner invitation that didn't include Cara. Assuring Jenny that she didn't mind, Cara had breathed a sigh of relief at the thought of a safe taxi ride instead of the usual wild ride she could expect if Rick was at the wheel.

Before leaving her Greenwich Village apartment for the short trip to the hotel where the dance was being held, Cara had taken one last look at herself in the full-length mirror on the back of the bedroom door. Jenny's genius as a dress designer was apparent in the witch costume she had created. The bodice was misty black organza over black silk, fitted to her beautifully shaped breasts and narrow waist. The neckline was cut in a wide V which exposed the contour of her bust and elegant line of her collar bone. Long tight sleeves that barely capped her shoulders ended in points just above the shapely fingers of her graceful hands. Made of large diamonds of sheer black organza, the skirt moved in eddies about her legs, parting here and there with the motion of her walk, revealing and concealing her long limbs which were delicately shadowed by gossamer black panty hose.

As Cara examined herself in the long mirror, she was aware that her loose flaming red hair was in direct contrast with the tightly drawn topknot that was her every-day style. For the first time in months she had used makeup—pearly green eyeshadow and blue black mascara—and her eyes appeared more vividly blue green than usual. More at ease in jeans or corduroy pants with loose cotton shirts or baggy sweaters, Cara felt a stranger to the enticing vision she saw reflected back at her. For a moment she thought of not going to the dance. Jenny and Rick would forget about her in all the excitement. But then, with a sudden toss of her head, she picked up her cape and draped it over her shoulders.

She had no trouble flagging a cab even though there was a slight drizzle. Nine o'clock on a Saturday night was usually the most impossible time of the week to find an empty taxi, but luck was with Cara. There was a passenger just leaving a cab at the entrance to her building. Quickly she tucked herself into the interior of the car and gave the driver the destination. With a slight skid, he pulled away from the curb and picked up speed as he turned into LaGuardia Place.

"It'll be fastest if I take Houston Street, lady . . . then we can turn up Sixth without any trouble." The driver met her eyes in the mirror. "Is that O.K. with you?"

"Sure. Just take it easy. You've got a nervous back-seat driver here." Cara laughed as she answered him. "I just want to get there in one piece."

"O.K., lady. It ain't often that I carry a witch on Halloween, so I'll be real careful. Guess your broomstick is outta wack, huh?"

"You noticed my hat!" Cara touched the black cone that sat atop her head. "And I thought I was disguised!" She smiled at her unusual garb. It had been a while since she had felt so carefree. Donny's long illness had prevented any social excursions for the year and a half before his death. That time, and the two years of her widowhood, was like years lost from her life. Jenny was right—it was time for her to forget the hurt and loneliness and start living again.

The sudden lurch of the subway car reminded her of the skidding movements of the cab as it had moved through the damp streets. There had been a sudden pileup of traffic, one of the usual hazards of New York City driving. This time, when the driver put on his brakes, the thin film of oil that had risen to the surface of the road caused a more serious skid. The driver had been helpless as the cab plowed into the car in front of him, throwing Cara forward. While the cabbie recovered from the collision, Cara found her slightly dented hat and righted herself, examining her gown and hose to see that they hadn't been torn.

"Hey, lady, are you all right?" The driver's voice had been anxious. "Gosh, I'm sorry, my brakes didn't do no good, but it was because of the wet street . . . must have been an oil slick. You look kind of wonked. Are you sure you're O.K.?"

"Don't worry, I'm all right. Just a little shaky, but that'll pass." Cara lay back against the cool vinyl seat, more shaken than she wanted to admit. "By the time you've got everything straightened out with the other driver, I'll be fine."

"Well, hold on a minute, I've got something that'll fix you up in no time." He pulled a thermos bottle from under the front seat and uncapped it. As he poured a stream of brown liquid into the thermos top, the smell of coffee reached Cara. "Now all it needs is a little medicine . . ." He poured another liquid into the cup and handed the concoction to Cara. "Here, just drink this right down and it'll set you straight. It's called Irish magic!" He winked at her before he moved away from the cab. "I gotta get the other guy's number, then I'll have us over to the Sheraton in no time . . . just take it easy now." The cabbie attended to the necessary details as Cara sipped the brew. The heavily sugared coffee masked the taste of the potent whiskey that the cabbie had liberally added to the mix. Cara, unaccustomed to alcohol, appreciated only the warming quality of the beverage, unaware of the effect it was to have on her.

She arrived at the hotel to find an anxious Jenny and Rick waiting for her. Without stopping to listen to an explanation of Cara's late arrival, Jenny hustled her off to the lady's room, shooting instructions at her as they went. Feeling like a teenager being coached by an overconscientious mother, Cara nodded her head in response, knowing that until Jenny ran out of steam there would be no stopping the flow of verbiage.

"Jenny . . . Jen!" she finally began once her room-mate's mouth stopped moving. "I'm a big girl now, you don't have to worry." Suddenly she reached out to grab onto Jenny's arm, "Oh my . . . hold on a minute, Jen, I . . ." Limply she leaned against the smaller woman.

"Cara! What's the matter? You look as white as a ghost!" Jenny's words expressed the concern in her eyes.

"It's all right . . . the cab I was in was involved in an accident and I think I'm still a little woozy. I felt dizzy for a minute, that's all." Cara straightened up, the momentary vertigo over. "As long as we're here, let me use the mirror to fix my lipstick . . . I think I ate most of it on the way."

"You could use some, and maybe a touch more blusher, otherwise you look sensational. That dress really does things for you, even if I do say so myself." Jenny eyed her creation with pride. "If only I could sign it like a painter signs a painting . . ." A wistful tone crept into her voice.

"That's O.K., Jen, I'll advertise the designer. But when you become the greatest theatrical costume designer in New York, don't forget you owe me. I want front row seats for every show you dress!" The two women smiled at the fantasy as Cara adjusted her makeup. "But before we go any further, what was the rush to get me in here? Knowing you, I'm sure it wasn't because of my pale cheeks. You have that look of 'let's have a heart-to-heart'!" Cara tucked her makeup into the little gold leather bag she carried. "What are you so eager to tell me?"

"Oh, it's so exciting, Cara—someone told me that Quinn Alexander is going to be here. He's one of the judges."

"One of the judges? Of what? And who is Quinn Alexander?"

"Who is Quinn? . . . You must be joking, and you about to enter the profession of space planning and interior design! Honestly, Cara . . . where have you been for the last year and a half?" Jenny's eyes were wide with astonishment. "He's just the publisher of the top magazine in the field . . . and on a scale of one to ten, he's an eleven!" She laughed and a teasing glint appeared in her eye. "It's a good thing I'm seeing Rick or I'd put that one on my 'most wanted' list."

"So?"

"What do you mean 'so?' I'm going to introduce you to him. I met him when he made a whirlwind tour of the school a couple of weeks ago. Now I'll just point out your costume to him, taking credit for it, and introduce him to you at the same time. You can take over from there!"

"I don't know, Jenny. I think I'd rather just enjoy myself this evening . . . kind of mingle with the people I know. I don't think I really feel up to meeting new people, especially VIP's like this Quinn person."

"Don't worry about it, Cara, it'll be as easy as falling off a log. All you'll have to do is stand and look beautiful and the costume will do the rest." Without giving Cara a chance to contradict her, Jenny led the way out of the restroom.

The pulsating sounds of the rock band surged through the wide gilt-trimmed doors of the ballroom and the party-goers were streaming into the dimly lit room. Strobe lights flashing purple, blue and red reflected from the scintillating mirrored globes that moved above the dancers. An occasional spotlight picked out figures dressed in everything from fig leaves to baroque costumes to futuristic geometric outfits. Glittering silver fabrics, gold paillettes and rainbow colored sequins shimmered in the dim light, confusing the eye and lending a hint of *Walpurgisnacht* to the scene.

As she sat tiredly in the moving subway, Cara recalled being introduced to several interesting young men. At first she had wanted to run from their admiring eyes, but then she began to feel an exhilaration that was like champagne in her blood stream. She was no longer quiet Cara Williams, widowed student; she was a mysterious, glamorous witch endowed with unknown abilities and charms and tonight was hers!

She had put her arm around Jenny's waist and with a wicked smile had agreed to Jenny's suggestions. "Don't worry about me, Jen," she had said, "I plan on being the belle of the ball. Just bring on the ogre, and I'll do my best to tame him!"

Jenny had looked startled at her change of attitude, but finally nodded and moved away with a saucy wink.

Cara had been swept to the dance floor by a thin Mephistopheles who twirled her around and then began to gyrate to the beat of the drums. Cara's hair swirled in a red cloud as she kept time to the music, her quick movements matching the pulsing sound around her. She was unaware of the gaze of a tall, dark-haired man, his eyebrow raised in appreciation of the lissome body and vivid hair.

No sooner had the number ended than she had been captured by a dashing Spanish Hidalgo and led into the seductive rhythm of a tango. She had surprised herself with the complete freedom with which she was responding. For the first time in years, she accepted what was happening with a carefree enjoyment, caring only for the moment, giving no thought to anything other than the immediate present. Her bewitching green eyes and sparkling smile encompassed everyone; but it was an answering smile from an extraordinarily handsome man that caught her eye. His gaze was so intense that she was drawn to it, wondering who he was and if she would be meeting him. Unlike most of the other party-goers, he was in black tie rather than a costume.

As the room became more crowded and the temperature increased, her thirst took her to the punch bowl more frequently. She had been careful to drink only the fruit punch; she knew she had no head for liquor. But she had missed seeing the wicked grin on the face of the freckle-faced prankster who emptied bottles of vodka into the beverage. She had noticed that she was feeling more relaxed as the evening progressed and enjoying herself as never before.

She had just finished dancing a rock number with Rick when Jenny grabbed her hand and dragged her over to the tall, dark-haired man who had been watching the crowd with a sardonic look on his lean, hawkish face. It was the man she had noticed, the one whose eyes wouldn't let her go.

"Oh, Mr. Alexander," Jenny's voice rang out. "Hi . . . remember me? We met last week when you were making the rounds at the Institute."

A smile that was a mere quirk of the lips acknowledged Jenny's presence. "Certainly, Miss . . . Miss . . . ?" The black eyes studied Cara.

"Jenny Davis, Mr. Alexander. I just wanted you to see the costume I designed. My friend Cara Williams is wearing it . . . This is Cara and this is the costume." Jenny pulled Cara next to her, refusing to heed the reluctance that held Cara back.

"Jenny, really." Cara felt almost giddy as Quinn's eyes roved over her, examining the dress and its wearer with eyes that held a wicked gleam.

"Very nice, Jenny . . . and very, very nice, Miss Williams!" A dark eyebrow lifted mockingly, "I've never seen a redheaded witch before, is your magic the white or black variety?"

A kind of madness seemed to take over Cara's normally retiring personality as she returned Quinn's look with a sidelong glance. "That depends on the circumstances, Mr. Alexander. . . ." For some inexplicable reason, her surroundings seemed to fade and the dark-eyed face became the focal point of her attention.

"Oh please, make that Quinn. I don't want any formality between us, Cara." As he spoke he reached for her hand and skillfully drew Cara onto the dance floor before she could deny him the privilege. "Just what circumstances did you mean?"

She answered with a shrug of her shoulders, relax-

17

ing into the haziness that was beginning to dim her senses. She did not want to fight this attraction that threw her cool self-control out of kilter.

He had been very adept, she remembered, both on his feet and with his words. She had felt a delicious tremor somewhere in the pit of her stomach as he pulled her against him, tucking the hand he held behind her at waist level, forcing her breasts against his chest. Without volition, she had begun to caress his head, fingers stroking his dark crisp curls. The swooping, melodic music matched the excitement within her as she moved to the rhythm of the dance, answering the pressure of his hand on her back. Their bodies fit together as though made for each other, leg following leg, hip against hip, eyes locked in soundless communication.

Lightheaded with the excitement of the moment, Cara flirted daringly with the man who held her tightly in his arms as they drifted slowly to the romantic strains of the music. Her hand was held captive in his as his other hand moved possessively across the small of her back, baring the satin smooth skin still slightly tanned from the summer sun. His touch sent shivers of rippling delight down her spine.

"You've bewitched me, Witch," he'd murmured as he tightened his arms around her. "I don't think I want to let you go. You feel too good in my arms."

She had been unable to answer him as the surrounding scene began to blur in and out of focus. She felt herself needing the support of his arms, leaning against his strong body.

"I feel as though I'm going to float away, Quinn," she whispered, resting her head against him.

"Then we'll float together, Witch. I never want to let you go. I'll call my magic carpet and we'll go wherever you want . . . in or out of this world." She felt his lips against her temple, sending a quiver of sensation through her body.

"I'd like that," she murmured dreamily. "Let's go someplace warm and soft and gentle. . . ." She gave a small chuckle. "It's so funny, my eyes can't decide whether they're open or closed."

The spiked punch had begun to take effect. Cara was as yet unaware that the seemingly innocuous fruit drink had been liberally laced with vodka. The punch, in addition to the restorative drink given her by the cabbie, had been enough to break down the wall she had built around herself after her husband's death. Her body was beginning to assert its needs; her inhibitions had been swept away.

She couldn't understand why or how she had suddenly become so uninhibited—she had literally tumbled into Quinn Alexander's arms. Parts of the evening were blurred, but other parts . . . She remembered his arms around her. Oh yes, she remembered that. And she remembered leaving him to dance a wild Spanish dance with a friend from design class. They had been the center of an admiring circle of people who applauded and cheered when she sank to the floor in a deep curtsey, giggling when she was unable to rise without the support of Quinn's hand.

He had taken her into his arms once more when the music started again, studying her in the flickering light, then leaning toward her to place a series of kisses along her jaw. She had lifted her chin to allow him free access to the sensitive skin of her neck, wanting him to continue the teasing movements with his mouth. He was satisfying a need within her that she had for too long refused to acknowledge.

"I'd swear you were drunk if I didn't know that you haven't had anything but punch to drink, beautiful one. Do you always get high on dancing?" he whispered in her ear.

"It's not the dancing," was her reply. "I've just been reborn . . . after years and years of being locked in a bottle like a *Djinn;* you unlocked the seal and here I am . . ." She moved her head, tossing the rippling flames of her hair. Her green eyes tangled with his, watching helplessly as they came closer and closer until, no longer able to take the weight of his glance, her eyelids drifted closed. His lips met hers, exerting just enough pressure to part them so that his tongue could pay tribute to hers, sending a searing message to her body. Her breath caught in her throat at the unexpectedness of her body's response and she suddenly realized she wanted that kiss to go on forever.

He lifted his mouth from hers, more aware than she of their surroundings. "Not yet, Witch, but soon. You're captivating me, my red-haired beauty . . . be patient."

He continued to guide her around the floor in time to the music, and she mindlessly followed his lead. When the music ended he whirled her away from the crowds, moving to the coat room for their wraps. "It's time to go, Witch, let's find that carpet and fly away home." The crooked smile said "I want you, come with me."

By the time he had draped her cape over her shoulders, the blur had changed to a pinkish glow. All she could remember with any clarity were the shivers that overcame her body when he placed a series of butterfly-soft kisses along the nape of her neck. His arms had wrapped the cape around her, holding her close to him as her heart tried to leap from the confines of her chest. She felt as though she had come home; here in his arms was her nesting place, all she had ever hoped or longed for. When he slowly turned her around, studying her face intently, letting his eyes linger on her lips, she felt as though the greatest adventure of her life was about to begin. Through the haze she knew she needed this man; she would not and could not deny him or herself anything.

She had been aware of nothing but the well-shaped mouth, at once sensitive and masterful, hovering above her own. She had reached toward it, as a flower reaches toward the sun, and sighed with satisfaction when later, his lips once more touched hers. If she could have described her feelings, she would have said she was falling in love.

Despite the tumultuous emotions sweeping through her, a remnant of sanity suggested that it was time for her to go home. She knew enough to realize that her common sense was weakening. For a moment she had been afraid, afraid that her better self would win and she would ask to be taken home. Softly she had laughed at the thought and when Quinn's face shot her a questioning glance, she had all she could do to keep her secret. Instead of voicing her request, she had taken his arm and said something about needing an extra large carpet for the two of them to ride on.

"Shall we stop at my place for a nightcap?"

She remembered those words because she could

hear herself objecting mildly. She had been unable to refuse his suggestion when he challenged her, telling her he must have been mistaken in thinking beautiful witches were brave and unafraid of convention. He had been a powerful magician to have made her lose every bit of control as she had.

The train pulled into the 59th Street station and Cara moved mechanically, still feeling out her memories of the preceding night. Now, too late, she was able to pin down the cause of her indiscretion. She had been as infatuated as an inexperienced sixteen-year-old. But still . . . she should have behaved with more control. Knowing why she had been so foolhardy didn't excuse her actions. Now she would have to live with them . . . and hope that this infatuation would pass. She had no hope of seeing Quinn again; their lives followed very different paths. Without the fuel of his presence, the fire in her blood would soon go out.

Cara stood in the station waiting for the Double R train, involved in memories that still flooded her mind.

There had been a long gray limousine waiting for them at the hotel entrance, driven by a blank-faced chauffeur who had opened the door for them. They had climbed into the spacious passenger compartment, luxuriously upholstered in gray with a telephone, concealed bar and small hanging nosegays on either side of the rear window.

The mist that had enfolded her mind the previous night had blurred the enigmatic quality of her escort's smile at her obvious bewilderment when she saw the chauffeur-driven car. With a raised eyebrow, he had explained it as a fringe benefit, asking if she objected to luxury. She had chuckled as she told him his magic carpet didn't have a fringe. Then she had let her body sink back against the upholstered seat. Her sigh of contentment attested to her appreciation of the automobile.

"I love it," she grinned. "Anytime I can get a ride on a magic carpet like this, I grab it. That's why I want to thank you for taking me home."

"No, no," he interrupted. "Thank *you* for allowing me to take you home. I wouldn't want to end the evening without you." He took her hand in his, then raised it to his lips, touching the sensitive palm with the tip of his tongue. "You asked me to take you someplace warm and soft and gentle. How could I refuse a request like that?—especially from someone so beautiful." He lifted Cara's hand to his cheek as his other arm encircled her waist, pulling her close to him. Her head tilted back against the gray fabric, her green eyes wide with apprehension and anticipation. Slowly he lowered his mouth to hers, touching her lips softly, then with a forceful passion that immobilized her defenses. Her mouth opened in surrender, her tongue answering his. Her hand moved to touch the back of his neck, crept up into his hair, needing to excite him as she was being excited.

Just as she thought she would drown in the tide of emotion, his mouth lifted away from hers. His voice broke into the moment, announcing that they had arrived at their destination and it was time for her to leave the cocoon of the car.

Her next recollection was of being in a rosewood-panelled elevator, a prisoner in his arms, laughing softly with elation. A part of her clutched at sanity, aware that she was playing a dangerous game, that she was too vulnerable. But the part of her brain that governed caution had been overridden by the fuzziness that had intruded all evening.

She had found herself in a beautifully furnished room overlooking the East River. Through the windows she could see the lights of the Queensborough bridge and in the distance, the flat, undistinguished darkness of Queens. The blinking lights of planes landing at LaGuardia and Kennedy Airports were visible in the darkness.

Released by the arms that had been supporting her, she kicked off her black satin and rhinestone sandals. The dark polished parquet floor had been cool to her feet but the coolness quickly changed to a soft warmth as she stepped onto the thick cream-colored Berber rug. She stood for a moment in an island of light cast by the hooded, arching lamp, unsure of herself in this strange place. But her uneasiness disappeared when Quinn's hands lightly touched her neck as he removed the cape from her shoulders.

She felt as though she were floating in a pool of sensual experiences: the softness of the rug, the silken touch of his hands, the harmony of the colors in the room, the fabric of her dress against her body. Everything added to the moment until her body felt as though it were drowning in a flood of tactile messages.

He had thrown the cape onto a chair, taking her in his arms, letting his lips nibble across the line of her shoulders and down to the hollow between her breasts. Breathless, she gasped at the piercing sensation caused by the pressure of his mouth. In the background the haunting passages of a favorite love song wove its own spell, drawing her further into the dreamlike cloud that had entrapped her earlier that evening.

Slowly he let her go, leading her to the deep, tobacco-colored couch, pulling her onto his lap as he sat down. He ran a finger across the line of her jaw and down the side of her throat, stopping at the tiny throbbing of her pulse. His hand slid to the back of her neck and he pulled her toward him; she felt his lips again, urgent and demanding her response. Her mouth parted and the tip of her tongue ventured forth, gently touching his mouth, feeling the shape of his lips, the velvet of his tongue as he entered the moist reaches of her mouth.

A wave of sensation started in her innermost being and kindled a million fires in her body. The give and take of this kiss was more intimate and erotic than any embrace she could remember. The moment held endlessly, until with a sigh Cara put her arms around the magician, wanting to hold and be held. Mindlessly she responded to the touch of his hands on her body, the slow saraband his fingers played on the bare skin of her arms and back. She moved closer to him, wanting to burrow into his warmth, relishing the moment.

Slowly his hands moved to cup her breasts, causing a moan as her body arched against his. His fingers delicately stroked her through the fabric of her dress and caused a burning that cried to be quenched by his passionate embrace. The movement of the zipper of her dress was a whisper directing her to shrug her shoulders so that the garment could fall away from the curve of her breasts, exposing them to his enticing, exciting caress.

Still captive of his mouth, she reached for the buttons of his shirt to find warm skin; the shirt was gone and her hand felt the beat of his heart. Her hands rubbed against the hair on his chest, across the muscles of his back, moving, moving, striving to give him the pleasure he was giving to her. She forgot that she was Cara Williams; that she had goals to achieve, a past she could not ignore. She had become a stranger living only for the desire and fulfillment of that moment. Time vanished and to her bemused mind it was as though she were once more in the arms of her first love, exploring and enjoying the pleasure each found in the other's body.

"Witch, my red-haired witch," sighed the voice against her mouth. His lips continued down the soft skin of her neck, pausing to drop little kisses along the way until he reached the tips of her breasts. Her nipples were hardened, ready for the next movement in the continuing dance of passion.

Her impressions came back like frames of a movie in slow motion. She saw her hair floating weightlessly about her head after he had disturbed the soft styling. He had helped her impatient hands undo buttons, pull at clothing, slip off garments. Then he had lifted her into his arms. He held her high, and placed kisses along her breasts, then down the midline of her body to her navel and the slight swell of her abdomen to the sensitive skin beyond. Her gasps of pleasure spurred him on to carry her swiftly to the room that held the huge bed, covers turned back, ready for its occupants. The pillows sank down as her head was lowered onto them. She saw herself reach out for the strong, virile body, as his head bent, his mouth taking an eternity to reach and taste the rosy tips of her breasts. She smelled his unique masculine scent as she buried her face in his neck, sighing at the reawakening of pleasure unknown for so long.

Lost in the memories of that passionate encounter, Cara let a train go by, unaware of its presence. Only when the next one entered the station did she realize her surroundings. Her body flushed with shame as she recalled the extent of her responses the previous night and she ran to the subway car, as if to escape these memories.

What kind of magician was he, this man who had been the instrument of her sensual reawakening? Perhaps it had all been a dream; but no, she hadn't dreamt waking up in that huge bed, lying next to his long lean body. She had dreamt about Donny, that she remembered—that she was in his arms, that it was he who had lightly traced the curves of her body with pleasure-giving hands, followed by warm kisses that aroused her as never before. She remembered a presence hovering above her, taking her to an ecstatic passion as she called out Donny's name. Then all was lost in darkness until she awoke next to a stranger.

She knew nothing of the stranger's frustrated anger when in her fulfillment she had cried out another man's name; she hadn't been conscious of the way he had thrust her away. Turning his back to her, his ego had been bruised when she called someone else in such an intimate moment. She knew he had evoked responses she had never known herself capable of; even now, half disgusted at herself for what she considered her wanton behavior, she relished the lingering memories of their passionate interlude.

She had arisen from that shameful bed, barely glancing at his sleeping face. Her face blushed, then paled, as she followed the trail of her clothes: panties, hose, gown and shoes spread from the bedroom into the living room, dropped carelessly, impatiently, across the floor. Even the combs from her hair . . . there had been two but she could find only one.

In an agony of embarrassment, Cara had dressed and hastily tidied her hair, wanting to leave the apartment before Quinn awoke to confront her. For a moment, she had been confused at not being able to find an entrance door, then realized that the exit was directly into the elevator. Obviously she was in a penthouse, but until she reached street level, she was not certain where the building was located.

Fortunately a subway station was less than a block away and she had a subway token in the tiny evening clutch she carried. The first glimmer of sunrise could be seen as she ran down the steps to the platform, holding her cape around her as though it would protect her from the consequences of her inexplicable behavior. She stood waiting on the platform, trying to put together the events of the preceding evening that had brought her to this moment, this anguish. What had happened to cause her to so forget her standards and wind up in a stranger's bed? A stranger named Quinn Alexander.

That they had been introduced made him no less a stranger. Nor did the fact that she had felt passion flare between them from their first exchanged glance. She had gone into his arms as though she belonged there, giving him the right to do as he wished with her.

Thank goodness she would never see him again; it would be too terrible to have to face the look that most certainly would be in his eyes.

Perhaps she would be able to understand her behavior once she'd had some sleep . . . She would think about it later . . . when she got home.

2

~~~~~~~~~~~~~~~~~

Wearily Cara unlocked the door to the apartment she shared with Jenny, shuddering at the thought of the questions she would have to answer. How was she going to tell her roommate about last night? It was inconceivable that she, Cara Williams, should have indulged in such wanton behavior. She could find no excuse for it—it was totally out of character for her. Unless she had become so . . . frustrated? No, impossible. But what would she tell Jenny?

Slowly Cara took off the rumpled costume and folded it away, moving quietly into the bedroom. To her unutterable relief Jenny was not in. She had probably decided to stay the night with Rick. Jenny had no qualms about spending the night somewhere other than her apartment. Besides, she and Rick had been going together for months. But for Cara, the idea of having an intimate relationship with any man other than a husband was foreign. Donny was the only man she'd ever slept with until last night, and they had married within weeks of having met. They'd been too young to want to wait, but Cara had needed the sanction of wedding vows before consummating their love. How different last night had been from the gentle sweetness of her honeymoon with Donny. She had unthinkingly given herself to a man she didn't know, an arrogant stranger. Remembering the explosive passion of their joining, she flushed uncomfortably—it was almost too much to bear.

She fervently hoped that they would never meet again; she would never forget those piercing, entreating eyes and that seductive, beautiful mouth. She hesitated to think what would happen if she fell under his spell a second time.

Jenny's empty bed reminded Cara that she would not have to explain her absence. It was the first tentative step in erasing the shattering events of the night. She took a hot shower, scrubbing her body repeatedly in an attempt to wash away her guilt. Exhausted, she wrapped herself in an oversized terry robe, dropped onto her bed and pulled the covers tightly around her. Although afraid that the confusion of her thoughts would prevent her from sleeping, she immediately fell into a restless sleep, filled with pictures of satanic black eyes gazing down at her in triumph. Her dreams were finally interrupted by the sound of pots and pans being rattled in the kitchen and the aroma of coffee wafting through the air.

"Jen, is that you?" Cara called as she rose from the rumpled bed, belting her robe securely around her waist.

"I'd like to know who else you think it might be!" Jenny responded saucily as she peered around the edge of the bedroom door. "You must have had some night, Cara, you look terrible. What happened to you? Rick and I looked for you when we were leaving but couldn't find you anyplace. Who brought you home?"

"Oh . . . I . . . I took a taxi. We must have missed each other in the crowd. I got tired and felt a little dizzy so I left."

"I'm glad. I know you were drinking the fruit punch and I was afraid that you might get drunk on it. We found out that Jack Davis spiked it with vodka. Did you ever? He really is something else. Rick was ready to beat him up . . . such a sophomoric thing to do. Some of the people who drank it got really bombed."

"I thought there was something wrong with the taste, and things did get kind of blurry." Cara was able to feel some ebbing of guilt, knowing she was one of those hapless few. She felt a modicum of comfort in the thought that her behavior had been the result of the release of her inhibitions because of the vodka. Then she remembered her responses to the skillful hands and mouth of her masterful lover and once more she felt a confused anger at herself and Quinn Alexander.

"You look hung over, Cara, are you sure you didn't drink too much of that stuff? C'mon into the kitchen and have some coffee. Rick left already and won't be back until later this afternoon."

Before Jenny could question her further about the preceding evening, Cara began to speak about Thanksgiving and plans for the holidays. She succeeded in eliciting a flow of chatter that needed little response. Murmuring sounds that could be interpreted however Jenny wished, Cara followed her into the tiny kitchen, avoiding any further explanation of her disappearance from the dance. The best thing she could do at this point, she reasoned, was to bury the whole incident. Just forget the man, the apartment and the night. Hopefully Jenny wouldn't take it into her head to pursue the matter, and with luck no one else would have noticed her departure from the dance.

The most important thing in her life right now was the remaining months of the semester. By January she would have her diploma and school would be behind her. She had known that the experience of returning to school at her age would be difficult; she wasn't young enough to be a part of the student body socially, nor old enough to be completely separate from it. But it would soon be over. In January she'd graduate and then she could get on with her career.

When Cara returned to her classes that Monday she waited for someone to make a remark about the Halloween party. But except for a few comments about the wild flamenco she had danced, she might never have been there. For a while she avoided the few friends who might have noticed her actions, but then, as the weeks went by and no one looked at her with questions in their eyes or made any kind of remark that might have had a double meaning, she began to relax. She had forced the picture of the fascinating face with the black eyes into the deepest reaches of her mind. For the first few days of November, she would jump at the sight of any tall, dark-haired man, but that, too, passed as she became more involved with her end-of-term work.

Her free-lance project with Robert Avery kept her especially busy. She was basing her senior project on the renderings she was painting for the large Long Island home that was his current commission. In actuality she was his assistant on the job, researching new fabrics and furniture sources and coordinating the schedules of the many workmen involved in the restoration.

She and Robert were spending the Saturday afternoon after Thanksgiving at the mansion, checking over the previous week's work and matching furniture placement with Cara's drawings. They moved from one room to another, discussing the window treatments that would best show off the spectacular view of Long Island Sound, Robert holding one edge of the large floor plan and Cara the other. He had a hand on her shoulder and was standing companionably close while they studied the blueprint, when suddenly he began to speak about their relationship.

"We work very well together, don't we?" he said, squeezing her shoulder to accent his words. "I don't think I've ever enjoyed working with a woman so much. You have a great sense for the work that we do, and you don't become emotional every time we disagree over something."

Surprised at the turn in the conversation, Cara made a remark about the respect she had for Robert's ability as a decorator and professor. "After all," she continued, "you have a lot to teach me and I'm willing to be told when my ideas may be wrong. I don't give in all the time, Robert."

"You know Cara, I've been thinking a lot about us." His manner was less sure now.

"About *us?*" Slowly Cara began to roll up the large sheet of paper as she moved away from the slim, well-dressed man. She was quite sure that she wanted to avoid a proposal from him. "Uh . . . listen, Robert, do you think you could wait a bit, I'm really starving and I have a feeling that this is going to get too involved for me. I don't want you to say anything that might . . . you know what I mean . . . Oh damn! Let's go get something to eat."

"Well, if that's what you want to do." Seeing her discomfort, he changed the subject. "We still have a lot to do here. Mrs. Brent wants the place finished by February first and the furniture will be arriving in about three weeks. Really . . . I'm sorry, I hadn't realized that you weren't ready to talk about us." He reached out to her, taking the rolled up plan and then drawing her hand into the crook of his elbow. "Look Cara, it's O.K. We'll keep up the teacher-student routine for now. Just give me a hint when you're ready to talk partnership—of any kind—business, marriage or otherwise." He patted the hand he held captive, almost avuncular despite the implications of his words.

"Thank you, Robert, I appreciate the sentiment, but not yet. I wouldn't want to spoil our relationship!" Cara flashed a relieved smile at him, her green eyes conveying the gratitude she felt at his understanding manner.

She truly didn't want to upset the equilibrium that

existed between herself and Robert. He had been a good friend; but that was all that would ever bind the two of them—friendship. His touch, his gentle kiss did nothing to raise her blood pressure despite the fact that she had come to rely on his presence in her life. Now that he had given an indication of what his future plans were as far as she was concerned, she had better find some way to defuse their relationship and shift it from social to business. She liked him too much to hurt him, but she could see no other way; at least until he was firmly convinced that there was no future for them.

Several minutes later the uneasiness that Cara had experienced faded and she was once more able to fall into the relaxed banter that was their usual mode of communication. When he asked her to spend the following day with him she put him off; he knew the flurry of assignments that had to be finished before the end of the semester and accepted her excuses easily.

Early in December, the Interior Design Department had a showing of the work of senior students in the college art gallery. On display were drawings of beautifully furnished living rooms, dining rooms, studio apartments, offices and community service areas. Included in the exhibit were detailed scale models of rooms built from balsa wood, Styrofoam and plastic. Photographs of finished designs accompanied sample boards showing drawings or pictures of furniture with swatches of the fabrics, rugs and wallcoverings to be used. It was an astonishing presentation, showing the scope of talent that was the sum total of the graduating class.

Cara had been asked to do an article detailing and evaluating the show for the school newspaper. Her piece would also be used in *Domestic Design,* one of the leading magazines in the interior design field. Her breezy style of writing combined with the meticulous attention she paid to details earned her the attention of the Dean of Students, Dr. Elliot. Shortly after she had submitted the article to the newspaper, she received a note in her mail folder requesting her presence in his office.

"Oh, Cara, I'm glad you were able to come so quickly," was his greeting when his secretary had shown her in. "I wanted you to know how pleased I was with your article on the senior showing. Very well done. In fact good enough to have brought you to the attention of the editor of *Domestic Design.*" He watched her, waiting for her reaction.

A flush of pleasure touched her cheeks. It wasn't often that the dean personally conveyed his respects to students.

"Thank you, it was an easy piece to write. There was so much good work on display that the only difficulty was trying to decide what *not* to include!"

"I can understand your difficulty. I spoke to Professor Avery the evening of the opening party and mentioned the high quality of the work." He gestured her to a seat as he returned to the deep leather desk chair. "What are your plans following graduation? Do you have anything definite in mind?"

"I have a few interviews set up, but so far the only concrete offer I've had is with a furniture showroom and I don't really want to go into sales, at least not in a showroom."

"Have you thought of combining your design knowledge with your writing ability?" The dean fiddled with his pen as he questioned her.

"I never really thought much about it. I always thought in terms of becoming a decorator. I love the challenge of a difficult room or a limited budget." Cara smiled as she followed her statement with a little shrug, saying, "The only problem is that I'm not so sure I can bring myself to like all my potential clients. In the year or so that I've been working with Robert Avery, I've met one or two who have been quite difficult to work with."

"Ummm, I know what you mean. Some people want a designer to tell them exactly what to do with their homes and then seem to take fiendish delight in insisting on impossible changes after the plans are drawn up." The white-haired administrator paused before continuing. "I called you here for a reason, Cara. Jake Harding, the editor of *Domestic Design,* called to ask if you would make an appointment with him for an interview. A position just opened up on the magazine and it was his feeling that you have the right qualifications. Are you interested?"

"Oh, yes. How fantastic!" Cara's face beamed with delight. "You mean Mr. Harding himself called?" At the dean's nod, Cara stood, her elation at this unexpected opportunity requiring some physical outlet. "When do you think he'll want to see me? Do you think I can handle the assignments? Oh . . . how marvelous! What an exciting thing to happen. I can't believe it!"

Dr. Elliot leaned back, smiling at her reaction. "Of course I think you can handle the work, I wouldn't have told you about the offer if I didn't. Jake wants to see you as soon as possible. He knows you won't be able to start full time until graduation two weeks from now, but he wants to get everything settled before then. Now, would you care to use my phone?"

Cara hesitated before she spoke again. "Who else would I have to see besides Mr. Harding? And why would they want me? I'm not a journalism major."

"My dear young woman, you produced a lucid, exciting article on the design show. Jake saw the copy that was submitted for use in the magazine, and he was impressed. You are knowledgeable about furniture, both historical and contemporary; you are familiar with fabrics and accessories and your color sense is practically perfect. In addition, you know all the big names in the business and express yourself intelligently and with a good deal of style. How could he possibly want anyone else?

"As for other interviews, you'll probably have to meet Quinn Alexander, the publisher, but that will be a mere formality since he has never yet disagreed with a choice of Jake's. Now would you like to use the phone?" Without waiting for an answer, Dean Elliot picked up the receiver, dialed a number, then handed the instrument to Cara, smiling benignly at the young woman whose heart had plummeted to her toes at the mention of that name.

3

Aren't you excited at the idea of working for Quinn Alexander, Cara? And to think I introduced you to him myself at the Halloween dance. What a coincidence!" Jenny carefully outlined her upper eyelid with eyeliner as she spoke. "I thought he was going to eat you up when he saw you. I think he likes redheads more than a little. Didn't he dance with you?"

"I don't remember . . . for I danced with so many people that night." Cara had turned away from Jenny's sharp eyes and was moving into the tiny hall of their apartment as she spoke. A coldness had begun to grow in the pit of her stomach; the thought that she would have to see her mystery lover again stunned her. What would she see in his eyes when they met? Would he expect her to fall into his arms again or would he ignore her? She didn't know which would be worse.

Jenny's comments continued: "I don't know how you could forget him. He's not the sort of man who fades into a crowd." The tone of her voice made it clear she was not buying Cara's disinterested manner. "You know, they say he's been married but his wife ran away with another man. It happened years ago, but he's been carrying a grudge against women ever since. Not that it stops him from having plenty of affairs, he just won't settle for one girl. And let me tell you, he's had plenty of women trying to tie him up in knots!"

"Ummm, yes, I suppose so," Cara answered blandly. "I doubt I'll see much of him if I get the job. Do you think I should look businesslike or feminine for the interview?" The question was sure to change the focus of Jenny's conversation. "I could combine my gray flannel jacket with that plaid skirt I bought last week, or I could wear the plum-colored silk shirtwaist dress. What do you think?" Talk about clothes always distracted Jenny and some sort of distraction was essential. As long as Jenny continued to think her roommate was completely disinterested in the man, she wouldn't delve into the events after the dance.

"Oh, wear the shirtwaist. It's a more sophisticated look. If you're going to be representing the best magazine in the field, you've got to look the part, or at least let them know that you can!" Jenny followed Cara into the kitchen. "Now, on the next question. Do you want a casual look with a scarf around your neck or a dressier one with lots of chains?" She tilted her head as she examined Cara. "I'd go for the elegantly casual look if I were you. You could wear that challis scarf you got for your birthday. The gray background

41

is neutral and the print has some plum in it. And wear those gold button earrings and your gray suede boots. They'll feel honored that such a fashion plate has allowed them to interview her!"

The thought that an influential editor like Jake Harding would be inclined to such an absurd reaction brought forth a delighted laugh from Cara, dissipating the fearful notions that had been running through her mind. It was all so silly. Most likely the man had forgotten her before he woke that day. If Jenny's gossip were to be believed, she had probably been just one in a series of bedmates. That thought didn't make her feel any better, but at least it left her feeling almost anonymous. She might not even have to meet him professionally. He spent so much time socializing that in all likelihood he was rarely at his office.

As she rationalized away her fears, Cara continued to discuss her coming interview with Jenny. Their conversation touched on the preparation of her portfolio, the possible inclusion of the renderings she had done for Robert and the article she had written as a class project. Cara found herself steering clear of the topic that she most wanted to discuss: how she was to react to Quinn Alexander. Jenny was still unaware of the events following the Halloween dance; something in Cara resisted the need to discuss her actions with another woman. The complete sequence of events was still a blur, but the shock of finding herself in the bed of a man to whom she had just been introduced was still present. Her behavior had been so unlike her normal standards that she could handle it only by ignoring it.

"What time do you have to be there?" Jenny's

question broke into the inconsequential patter that had been coming from Cara's mouth. "Will you have time to let me do your hair? I think you should wear it in a chignon . . . very chic, you know? I'd just tease it a little for some height and leave a couple of love curls dangling in front of your ears."

"Love curls? I'm going for a job interview not a proposition!"

"Oh, you know what I mean, you nut. C'mon, Cara, let me do your hair for you."

After a little more cajoling, Cara let Jenny style her hair and was pleased with the results. The coolly elegant young woman who presented herself at the offices of *Domestic Design* later that day held little resemblance to the bewitching, exciting creature who had danced a mad flamenco on All Hallow's Eve.

With a smile, the receptionist told Cara that Mr. Harding would be with her in a moment. The time seemed to crawl as Cara nervously reviewed the points she wished to bring to Harding's attention concerning her past experience and present capabilities. She knew she had more than a fair chance of getting the job since he had requested her presence. However, there was always the possibility of a personality conflict or some unforeseen hitch that would persuade him she was unsuitable as a prospective employee.

"Mr. Harding will see you now, Miss Williams."

"It's 'Mrs'."

"Oh, sorry, Mrs. Williams. Through that door, second on the left."

With a brief thanks and firmly crossed fingers, Cara made her way to the teak door, taking a deep breath before she turned the knob to Harding's office. Positive thinking, she admonished herself, think positively.

A slightly corpulent, gray-haired man sat behind an old-fashioned oak desk littered with folders, magazines and loose papers. Heavy eyebrows shaded bright blue eyes that were crinkled by his welcoming smile.

"Come in, come in, Mrs. Williams." The editor stood and moved from behind the desk as he spoke. "I've been looking forward to telling you in person how much I liked the article you wrote. You have a nice clean way of expressing yourself."

"Why, thank you, Mr. Harding. I was writing about something I really enjoyed. I think that was a big help."

"Let's sit down on the couch. My secretary fixed some coffee; how do you take yours? With or without cream?" Affably, the man gestured Cara toward a blue tweed couch. Once she was settled comfortably, he handed her a mug of coffee before sinking into the cushions at the other end of the sofa.

For a few minutes they spoke of neutral subjects. Then Harding led the conversation around to the important discussion of her qualifications and the requirements of the job.

After a half hour of questioning her, Harding made Cara a formal offer. He qualified it by announcing that she would of course have to meet with the publisher for final approval.

"The publisher?"

"Quinn . . . Mr. Alexander." A gray eyebrow raised questioningly. "I thought you knew him."

"Yes, we have met, but I . . ." Cara could feel a

rising heat in her cheeks. "It was my understanding that you had asked for me because of the article you saw. That's what Dr. Elliot said."

"And that's true, but all upper level appointments to the staff have to have Quinn's final approval. Not that there'll be any problem about you, Cara, he just wants you to meet with him before leaving the building."

"Upper level appointments?"

"Why yes, I thought you understood, Cara. With your background and experience you're going to be directly involved in the special feature we'll be instituting in our May issue, the Home of the Month article. It's Quinn's baby, but he's too busy to handle it beyond the first two that are planned. We're going to do a cover story each month about decorating problems that call for unique solutions. Some will be for very wealthy people and others for those with only a modest income. In the case of the latter, *Domestic Design* will be offering the services of their resident designer—you—to solve the problems in return for the right to show 'before' and 'after' pictures with the decorating budget, etcetera."

"It sounds fabulous, but I had no idea that the job entailed so much responsibility. I never expected a byline so soon!"

"Well, Quinn wanted a fresh outlook, so your lack of professional experience is a plus in this case." Harding put his mug on the coffee table in front of the couch. "You can discuss this all with him. He expects you in his office right about now."

"Oh, but I . . . I'd like to think about this. I . . ." Cara floundered for a way to express her reservations about taking the job. Then, mentally calling herself an idiot for even thinking of passing up an opportunity like this, she shook Harding's hand and thanked him for his time. "I'm very excited at the opportunity of working with you, Mr. Harding. I appreciate your giving me this chance."

A puzzled look crossed the editor's face. "Of course, I'm very impressed by your capabilities, but it was Quinn who brought you to my attention. I thought you knew."

"Quinn? But I hardly know the man." Well, that's true, Cara told herself, I don't *really* know him, not in a way that should influence my being hired as a writer. "Well, I suppose I'd better go and speak to him myself . . ." Her voice faded away uncertainly.

This was an unexpected complication. She had thought that Jake Harding had instituted the job offer; to find out that it was initiated by the sardonic figure who still haunted her nights was a real blow. Perhaps she should turn down the job and avoid the ensuing embarrassment of having to work with him.

"If you return to the reception area and take the elevator to the tower suite, I'll call and let him know you're on your way." Harding extended his hand in farewell. "It's been good talking with you, Cara. I know you're the right person for the job." He grinned as he shook her hand. "Life is going to be pretty hectic for you from now on!"

Smiling in agreement, Cara controlled the urge to run as she headed for the private elevator that would take her into the great man's presence. Why did he suggest me for the job? What is he expecting of me? Will he say anything? The questions spun dizzily in her mind as the elevator carried her to the forty-fourth floor of the building. She was hardly aware of the cessation of movement when the smooth ride ended. She was brought back to the present only when the stainless steel doors whispered open.

Now Cara, she addressed herself, you're a grown woman, you're not a teenager facing the unknown. Yes, but how to face him—how do I talk to him? Pretend it never happened, she answered herself, that you never met him. If he says anything about Halloween tell him about the accident and . . . and . . . the spiked vodka. Tell him you don't remember anything that happened from the time you were in the taxi until you woke Monday morning in your room. Now act your head off, girl.

She walked out of the elevator into a large oval room the color of cinnamon. The reception area was furnished with a large oval desk of burl elm behind which sat an exquisitely beautiful young woman dressed in an equally exquisite suit. Her lacquered elegance was matched by a bored, monotonous voice. "May I help you?" she asked.

"I'm Cara Williams," Cara announced. "I have an appointment with Mr. Alexander."

"Just a moment, Ms. Williams." The red tip of one finger pushed a button on the monitor board as she announced Cara's arrival in a muted voice. "Mr. Alexander's secretary will be here in a moment."

Just as Cara uttered her thanks, a well-dressed woman walked through the sliding doors behind the desk. "Mrs. Williams, Mr. Alexander is waiting for you in his office. Won't you come this way?"

As though I have a choice, thought Cara. Why do I feel as though I'm about to face the firing squad? He's only a man, isn't he?

Aware with all her senses of her surroundings, Cara paid silent tribute to the talent that had designed the suite of offices through which she was walking. Warm earth tones formed the background for stunning Italian contemporary furniture. Woods and suede, tweeds and burnished metal were used to create an aura of comfort that pleased the eye.

Cara was so busy looking at her surroundings that she was taken by surprise to find that the secretary had led her into Quinn's office. Only when she heard the woman's soft voice announce her name did she realize that the moment of truth had arrived. Slowly she brought her attention to the figure behind the massive desk, giving herself time to assume the cool armor that she hoped would protect her from his incredible charisma. To an onlooker, there was no indication that Cara had ever met Quinn Alexander before. No hint of the passion these two had shared could be discerned in their carefully impassive faces. The publisher casually thanked his secretary, then dismissed her with a request that coffee be served in half an hour. Almost as though to assert her independence, Cara requested tea instead, keeping her voice level, allowing no hint of the turmoil within.

As the door closed softly behind the woman, Quinn moved from behind the huge ebony desk to take Cara's elbow and conduct her to the seating arrangement in front of the broad picture window overlooking Fifth Avenue.

"Jake just called to tell me the interview went very

well. He feels sure you'll be able to handle the job without any problems." Before letting her sit down, the dark-haired man let his hands rest on her shoulders. "May I take your coat? You'll find yourself more comfortable without it."

Cara's green eyes flickered as she let the garment slide from her. "Thank you, Mr. Alexander."

"Oh please, no formality. We're a tight-knit group here at *Domestic Design* . . . first names only." A twitch of amusement moved his lips.

"Of course . . . Quinn." With an effort Cara managed to keep her voice vaguely pleasant. "I understand I have you to thank for the job. I do appreciate this opportunity and . . ." She was interrupted by his laugh.

"It's nice to see you again, Cara. You left before I could thank you."

His easy reference to their previous meeting was a blow that left Cara feeling nauseous. She paled slightly, hoping that the blusher she had so carefully applied that morning would hide her change of color. With iron control she raised her eyebrows in question. "Have we met before, Quinn? I don't remember . . . were you at the art exhibit at the Institute last month?" She felt the perspiration dampen the palms of her hands as she struggled to maintain her calm exterior.

"You don't remember? That's a little hard to believe." Quinn's eyes narrowed suspiciously. "We spent Halloween together."

"We spent Halloween together?" Cara echoed his words incredulously. "Are you sure?"

"Oh, quite sure. In fact, you left a little memento behind when you disappeared from my apartment."

He reached into his pocket and produced the jewelled comb that Cara had been unable to find that awful morning. "This *is* yours isn't it?"

"May I see it?" Cara couldn't believe that she hadn't started screaming, so uncomfortable did she feel in this situation. With an effort she extended her hand, controlling the tremors that shook her, and accepted the glittering adornment from her new employer. "It *is* similar to some that I have, but I don't see how you could have one that's mine."

"Do you want me to spell out the whys and wherefores?" His dark eyes were suddenly cold, hiding his thoughts.

"Mr. Alexander, this is very difficult for me." Cara refused to allow her anguish to intrude into her tone. "On Halloween I was involved in a taxi accident that shook me up quite a bit. On top of that, I drank a large quantity of fruit punch that I later learned was spiked with vodka. I'm afraid I have almost no recollection of the evening. All I know is that I found myself in my apartment Sunday morning without even knowing how I got home the night before. I lost some twelve hours out of my life and have no idea how I spent them." She twisted her slender hands together, turning the wedding band round and round on her finger. "If in that time I did or said anything that might have been misconstrued, I hope you will forgive me." She allowed herself to look into his expressionless face, trying not to betray her inner perturbation, hopeful that he would accept her story.

"And you don't remember anything of the intervening hours?" A note of incredulity was in his voice.

"Not a thing. It's been a worry, but in the two and a

half months since then there've been no repercussions, so I guess I didn't commit any crimes." She laughed lightly before she continued. "I hope you see now why I can't tell you for sure whether that comb is mine or not." She decided to attack, hoping that he would consider discretion the better part of valor. "Was there something significant about your having it?"

A light, either anger or amusement, seemed to flash in his eyes. "I thought it might have had more significance than it did. I probably made a mistake about it being yours."

Relief left Cara weak in the knees. She felt the seat cushion against the back of her legs and sank gratefully into the high-backed lounge chair, unable to hold herself upright any longer. The publisher seated himself in the chair opposite, stretching his long legs as he studied the woman opposite him. Cara glanced at him, noting the crease between his eyebrows, then bent her head to conceal the relief that must be evident in her face. Now, if she could keep up the charade, she would be able to work at the magazine without worrying about a confrontation with Quinn. Even if he weren't totally convinced by her story, he was puzzled. For the moment he would have to accept her explanation. By the time any further questions might arise in his mind she would have established herself at *Domestic Design* and his attention would undoubtedly be turned elsewhere.

Comforted by her thoughts, Cara came to with a start when she heard Quinn say, "We'll be making our first trip together next month. The September issue is going to feature the vacation home of Mr. and Mrs.

Howard Laketon just outside Ithaca on Lake Cayuga. I'd like you to get started on some quick sketches of possible decorative ideas for a year-round home with emphasis on the winter season."

"Our first trip? I don't understand." Cara's eyes had widened in shock.

"I thought you knew. You and I are going to be working quite closely together on these articles. I've made all the contacts and set up dates for the photo sessions preliminary to your starting your design work. But I want to follow the first few assignments from beginning to end, so we'll be traveling extensively together for the next few months."

Quinn's words were so unexpected that for a moment she was unable to respond. This was an impossible situation, she absolutely could not . . .

"What do you mean traveling together? I thought that this was to be my assignment?" Her voice wavered between doubt and indignation.

"Of course it's your assignment. No question about that." His answer was affable in the extreme, "It's just that you're a newcomer to the staff and I regard this as my pet project. Naturally, until I feel you're secure in your understanding of what I want . . ."

Cara looked at the blandly smiling face across from her, wondering if the words she heard really had a double meaning or if she was reading something into them that wasn't intended. It was almost impossible to judge, but she couldn't allow the possibility to exist. Quinn had successfully lured her into bed once before; she was going to make sure that she would not find herself there again.

"Mr. Alexander, I appreciate your desire to give as

much help as possible to a new staff member, but . . ."

"Not Mr. Alexander, Cara," the urbane voice interrupted. "I thought we'd settled the name thing." He leaned forward resting his elbows on his knees, his hands loosely clasped as he gazed intently at her. "You'll find that there's a great deal more to this concept than you think. I don't want you to have to deal with the personalities involved but you need to know them in order to design for them. Now, I happen to know the first two very well and can help you with their foibles. Trust me . . . you'll see. I want this to be very special. It's much too important to be mishandled." He leaned back in his chair, tucking a thumb into the watch pocket of his vest, daring her with his glance to deny the reasonableness of his point of view.

"Yes . . . well . . . Quinn." Cara's breath caught at the double entendre of Quinn's speech. "I hadn't really given too much thought to the requirements of the job, but I certainly didn't expect such a generous attitude from the publisher of such a top-notch publication. Isn't it unusual for someone of your standing to spend time on a tyro like myself?" Cara's temper was beginning to assert itself; unfortunately her response could also be interpreted in two ways.

"Not such a 'tyro,' quite proficient in fact." A reminiscent grin touched his face for a second, then disappeared as though never present. "Don't fight it, Cara . . . the Laketons are friends of mine. I talked them into this project because they've just bought a beautiful early Victorian home upstate and it presents some interesting problems. Now listen and learn, so you can start to research some ideas. That is if you don't already know everything about the period?" Suddenly his attitude was direct and businesslike, almost curt. "This is a couple who are involved in a number of sports: skiing, skating, swimming, tennis, whatever. They're active, intelligent, likeable and they want their home to reflect all this. They also plan to do quite a bit of entertaining. We'll spend five or six days there so you can absorb some atmosphere and then you'll have a month to do the drawings and design boards before we make the presentation. Technically, we have final say-so on the whole scheme, but we want our 'clients' to be happy with their new home, too." Quinn paused to check Cara's reaction to his plans. As soon as he had received a hesitant nod, he continued to describe the work. "And then," he finished, "the following month, while construction is going on in Ithaca, we'll be interviewing the Contessa da Villa Ruhia, for whom you are going to redesign the guest cottage on her Virginia estate. The contrast between the two pieces—one about a casual, all-American family, the other about a socially prominent Italian noblewoman—ought to promote reader interest. Since there's plenty of money involved in both lifestyles, there'll be plenty of glamor. And that's what your average person wants, plenty of glamor."

As Quinn spoke, outlining his plans for the new series, Cara studied his face, wondering if she were caught in a peculiar dream. Aside from one or two rather ambiguous statements, he had made no reference to their night together. It was true that he had tried to make something of the comb, but she had handled that quite well she thought. Her forthrightness in telling him about the accident had caught him off guard. If she wasn't so nervous she would have had a good laugh over that. The beast! She was not experienced with his kind, and would have to step carefully to make sure she stayed that way. A disturbing thought intruded into her reflections: was it possible that this job offer had something to do with that night? She caught her breath; the more she thought about it, the surer she was. This whole setup was too unusual to be anything else but that—a trap to catch her. Well, she'd be damned if she'd be caught. Mr. Alexander would have to look elsewhere for a pillow friend!

Quinn arose from his chair, unable to sit still any longer under what he perceived as the dispassionate stare of Cara's clear green eyes. For a sophisticated man of the world he found himself disturbed in the young woman's presence. Her manner was so correct, so formal, so impassive that he was forced to accept her amnesia story. Nonetheless, he found it almost impossible to believe that she had no memory of the exquisite passion they had shared. She had aroused and satisfied him as no other woman before; the uninhibited ardor with which she had returned his caresses, the beauty of her body, the eagerness with which she had enjoyed their stolen night was beyond his experience. She had been like a woman in love. Then he remembered further: she had called out a name at the moment her body shook with ecstasy and the name hadn't been his.

He turned his back to her and gazed out the window, suddenly obsessed with the desire to hear her murmur *his* name as she twisted and turned beneath him, sighing with passion. Once more he looked at her as she made some remark about his magazine. His sable eyes ranged over her curves, undressing her in his mind. The silk shirtwaist dress she wore faded away and he saw her as she had looked on his bed: rosy tipped white breasts, one long leg bent at the knee, eyes humid with desire. A glaze of perspiration broke out on his forehead and upper lip as his face paled. She really had bewitched him . . . unknowingly perhaps, but totally. He had a need to possess her again; to know whether his memory was playing tricks.

"Well, it sounds as though it could be a very exciting series. I don't recall any of the other home decorating magazines having done anything quite like this." Cara opened her portfolio. "If you'd like to see them, I have some sketches that I did for a restoration on Long Island. Maybe some of the ideas would be applicable?" She looked at Quinn with a question in her eyes which turned to concern as she saw his paleness. "Are you feeling all right? You don't look well. Can I get you a drink of water or anything?"

Quinn was startled out of the memories in which he had become lost. "No, thank you, I . . . uh . . . I'm just getting over one of those bugs that's left me with an occasional weakness. I'll be fine." He took his handkerchief from his breast pocket and dabbed at his forehead, wondering what had come over him. "I'd like to review your drawings with you, Cara, but I have another appointment in half an hour that calls for some preparation. Let's see, today is Thursday . . . why don't you plan on starting with us a week from next Monday?" His voice had become brusque, a sharp contrast to his earlier welcoming tone. He had planned on taking her to lunch, starting his campaign of seduction immediately, but he found he could no longer handle the powerful impulses that her presence aroused. "There's enough preliminary work to occupy you until we start traveling."

Cara studied the tall man once more, admiring the impeccable gray suit he wore, remembering the broad-shouldered body beneath it. Her breathing becoming unsteady, she pulled her eyes away from him. "That's fine. I have a few things that I have to take care of, a few loose ends to tie up before I start work here. When exactly do you want to go upstate?"

"We'll set the date once you've had a chance to settle in. There's no rush right now." He stood looking out the window, his back to Cara. "Before you leave, I'd like you to sign this contract. It's just a formality, but we have to be protected—all the publicity we'll be doing about the series and the projected articles. You understand, I'm sure. It's purely a formality. The agreement is made so that the two parties are committed—you to work for the minimum of three months, and the magazine to give you a minimum of three weeks notice of severance if the relationship is not mutually beneficial." He walked over to Cara, and handed her the legal document and pen.

Wanting only to bring this interview to an end, Cara grabbed both pen and paper and quickly signed her name on the indicated line.

"Don't you read before you sign?" His mobile lips quirked in a wry smile. "Or do you take everyone on trust?"

Flustered, Cara smoothed the gray leather gloves she held. "Of course not, but this seems cut and dried. Your company is reputable, I have Dr. Elliot's encouragement, so what could you have possibly included in the contract that could create problems for me?"

"In this case, nothing. But you shouldn't ever sign your name to anything without reading the fine print. You might find you've signed your life away!"

"Yes, well . . . I think I'd better leave now. It must be time for your next appointment." She stood up, reaching for her coat and scarf, ready to bring the encounter with this disturbing man to a close.

Once more composed and in control of his emotions, Quinn strode over to Cara, taking the gray coat from her hands. "By the way, do you ski?" he asked as he helped her into the garment.

"Why, I used to. I haven't for several years. My husband and I . . ."

"Your husband—where is he, Cara? I wasn't introduced to him when we met before." Once again there was the hint of ambiguity in his statement.

Wishing, for more reasons than one, that she could say Donny was at that moment waiting for her, Cara said without emotion, "My husband died two years ago, Mr. Alexander, that's why you weren't introduced to him." Quickly she pulled away from him. Feeling that she was treading on thin ice, she picked up her portfolio and handbag and moved to leave the plush office, pausing to say; "On second thought, Mr. Alexander, I'm not sure that the job is right for me. Could I have a few more days to think it over?" Her hand was on the door knob and she had begun to pull the door open.

"The time to think it over is past, Cara. You've signed the contract. I'll expect you here a week from Monday." A satisfied smile touched his lips.

Furious with herself and her new employer, Cara swung out of the office. If she could have, she would have slammed the door but the pneumatic hinge prevented her from venting her frustration. She brushed past the secretary's desk without hearing the other woman's congratulations on her new job. Blind with anger, she ignored the svelte receptionist and gratefully ran into the waiting elevator.

4

What have I let myself in for?" She spoke aloud in the empty elevator. "How could I have been so stupid, allowing myself to be talked into taking a job working with that . . . that . . ." She couldn't find a word to describe her feelings toward this man. "Travel with him. *Travel* with him! Damn, what am I going to do?" No calmer by the time the elevator reached the main level, Cara flagged a cab, wanting only to get home to the safety and privacy of her room.

As she sat in the moving taxi, she realized that it was time for her to talk with someone about the secret she shared with Quinn. She knew she wouldn't be able to work with him as long as she felt so guilty about the events of Halloween, nor would she be able to face her unwarranted response to him. But who could she talk to? Jenny was not very discreet and too romantic to be able to look at the incident clearly. Naturally talking to Robert was out of the question. If only she could talk to her Aunt Norma. Norma was close enough to her own age to understand, yet far enough away from the situation to be dispassionate. Maybe it would pay to fly up to Maine for the weekend. A breathing spell away from the city was exactly what she needed before her new job started.

By the time Cara had paid the cab driver, her plans were made. She called the airline and made a reservation for that same day, unconsciously wanting to extend her weekend for as long as possible. She could tie up loose ends when she got back. She pulled her green nylon duffle bag from the top shelf of her closet and quickly filled it with the items she would need. Without pausing, she took off the smart dress and boots, pulled on a pair of jeans, a bulky knit sweater and her boots. She removed the pins from her hair to release the sophisticated chignon, tying the glowing strands back with a green silk square.

After dashing off a short note to Jenny explaining her absence she was on her way to LaGuardia Airport and the important talk with Norma.

Despite the late January weather, the flight was uneventful; the landing at the Portland airport was made without a hitch. She rented a car and five and a half hours after her interview with Quinn she was pulling up in front of the blue cottage that was her aunt's home and pottery studio.

After parking the car in the driveway, Cara jumped out, grabbed her duffle bag and ran up to the front door. Now that she had made the trip to Kennebunkport, she was anxious to talk to Norma. In a way she felt like a young girl experiencing the bewilderment and confusion of her first infatuation. Her need to forget the events of Halloween evening, the repression of her responses to Quinn Alexander, and the continued feeling of excitement at the mere thought of the man, frightened her. She didn't know how to cope with these feelings and needed an impartial confidante.

Before she had a chance to ring the bell, the front door opened and her Aunt Norma stood there welcoming her with a wide grin.

"Cara, love, I'm dying to give you a hug, but I'm covered with clay up to my armpits. I certainly didn't expect to see you here before May. What's happened?" The smiling face leaned close and placed a warm kiss on Cara's cheek. "Your phone call was a big surprise, but you didn't explain why you wanted to come up so suddenly. Come on in. Put your suitcase in your room while I wash this clay off my hands. Meet you in the kitchen!"

Cara stood for a moment after Norma left the old-fashioned parlor, enjoying the warm welcoming feeling of the gracious antique-filled room. She had spent many happy hours visiting here when her parents had been traveling and unable to take her with them. There was a security in this house that Cara could not feel in the home that she had shared with her parents. Her father's work as an art dealer had taken him away on many weekends. On longer trips he had been accompanied by her mother; at those times Norma had become substitute mother, sister and friend, all in one.

She leaned against the wall, allowing the peaceful quality of the room to enfold her. The faded burgundy and gold stripes on the Duncan Phyfe couch, the handblocked linen drapes, the soft yellow Chinese lamps on the end tables, all filled a deep need for harmony that was present in Cara's makeup. She sniffed at the air, relishing the remembered scent of rose petal potpourri combined with the more acrid odor coming from the kiln in her aunt's basement studio. If she closed her eyes, she might almost be the sixteen-year-old who had come to spend the summer with her artist-craftsman relative. She had learned to love form and texture and color that summer, learned to see with the discernment of an artist's eye.

"The coffee's almost ready, love," her aunt's voice called. "Don't bother to unpack until later. Do you want a piece of gingerbread to go with the coffee?"

"I'll be right with you," Cara answered as she picked up her suitcase and went up the stairs to the guestroom. "I haven't eaten since breakfast, could I have a sandwich?" She dropped the bag just inside the door as she spoke, then turned back to walk downstairs and through the parlor to the spacious kitchen.

"I have some leftover roast beef, is that all right?" Norma was busily digging into the refrigerator. "Mayonnaise and lettuce? That's what you like with it, isn't it?"

"Uhmm, sounds perfect." Cara sat in the nook of the round oak-topped table, resting her clasped hands on it like a well-disciplined schoolchild.

Quickly her aunt prepared the sandwich and poured the coffee into handmade mugs, setting them down on the table with an accompanying sugar bowl and cream pitcher. As Cara hungrily bit into the thick sandwich Norma studied the faint shadows beneath the green eyes.

"You look a little out of it, Cara. What happened to send you running up here? I gather that whatever it is, you want to talk about it." The affectionate hazel eyes told the younger woman that whatever the problem, it would be met with understanding and loving regard, not a judgmental attitude. Whatever Cara needed, she could be sure of getting it from this woman.

Slowly she chewed her food, delaying her words for a moment longer, trying to clarify the exact story she wanted to tell. Finally, she swallowed, took a sip of coffee and then began.

"I'm in an awful muddle," she started, "and you're the only one who can help me straighten things out in my mind. You've always been my listening post and I really need you now." She stopped, searching for the right words, then began again. "Something happened to me a while ago and I'm very confused about the whole thing." Carefully Cara explained her abstinence from physical intimacy since the year before her widowhood and then went on to describe the events of October thirty-first, ending with the offer of a job at *Domestic Design* and the realization that the man who had once been her lover was now her employer.

"The crux of the problem is—that I don't know what to think about myself anymore. I feel as though I've done something . . . oh, I don't know . . . wrong, I suppose." In spite of the open relationship she had with her aunt, Cara was unable to look at her as she spoke. "Am I being stupid? And then there are the feelings of guilt because I . . . I . . . enjoyed him and I feel as though that makes me wicked and disloyal to my memories."

"Cara, my dear, there's nothing wrong with enjoying your body's responses. You're a normal female with normal desires." A soft laugh escaped the older woman's lips. "I'd be more worried if you didn't have these needs. In fact, I have been! It wasn't natural to lock yourself away. Now that the lock has been broken all those hidden feelings are tumbling out and they frighten you. Don't hold back because of that. You'll wind up a frustrated old lady, wrinkled and sour! I'm not telling you to go out and become a swinger—I don't think you'd enjoy promiscuity!" A gentle hand reached out to touch Cara's tilted head. "But don't run away because you're afraid."

The kitchen was quiet as Norma's voice died away. She pushed her chair back and got up from the table, walking to the stove to pick up the coffee pot, then changing her mind and putting it down again.

"Would you like some more coffee?" she asked Cara. "I think I'm going to have that piece of gingerbread. It's close to dinner but I just feel like a little nibble of something."

Cara was silent as she thought about her aunt's words, then slowly, reluctantly she said, "I'm afraid of what will happen when I start working with him."

"Yes, I gathered that. You're afraid that he may be too strong for you and that you may fall in love with him. Isn't that the problem?" She moved behind Cara putting her hands upon the younger woman's shoulders in an expression of loving concern. "I think what you really have to decide is whether you want to take the risk of coming to life—fully to life that is. You've buried yourself in your schoolwork, and I can understand your wanting to get the degree, but it's time for you to come out of that cocoon. You have a life to live, you've got a future ahead of you and that future should include relationships with men or a relationship with *a* man.

"You'll have plenty of time to think about what you're going to do next Monday. In the meantime you can just relax for the next few days and take it out on some clay!" Norma started to laugh. "You showed up at just the right time for me; I've a barrel of clay that needs wedging . . . a perfect opportunity for you to beat out all those feelings!"

"You know, Auntie mine," Cara smiled up at her aunt, "you really are a very special lady. Why is it that just hearing you speak so logically makes me feel better about everything? You're right, I *am* afraid of him. He's something else, Norma. I've never met a man like him . . . never." For a moment the smile faded. "But so what. He'll just expand my experience. And I'll learn to keep him at arm's length, or else!"

The long weekend with her aunt helped Cara to gain insight into her reactions to Quinn. She spent the time working in the studio and beachcombing along the waterfront talking with Norma. For the first time she was able to discuss her marriage and Donny's long illness and her feelings about herself and the world around her. She asked Norma about her own experiences and was able to appreciate the new openness with which the other woman answered her questions.

She returned to New York to attend her graduation

and put her affairs in order. By the end of the week she felt ready for any surprises that Quinn Alexander might throw at her—any, that is, except the one she found.

Early Monday morning she strode into the building that housed the editorial offices of the interior design magazine, prepared to learn the routine of her new job and to give it her best. When she arrived at the main reception area, she was directed to the tower floor where she had had her meeting with Quinn.

To her amazement, she was conducted to an office adjacent to his. She stood in the doorway stricken with astonishment. The office was decorated as though it were a plush living room; the walls, draperies and carpeting were a crisp peridot green. A tufted chesterfield couch covered in oyster white stria velvet was set against one wall fronted by a large round cocktail table. An exquisite arrangement of cymbidium orchids in an antique Rockingham bowl was centered on the table. Set in a semicircle opposite the couch were a pair of lounge chairs in striped green and white satin and a Chippendale wing back chair upholstered in peridot, white and pale coral tapestry. At right angles to the central window, with its view of Central Park, stood a fruitwood and mahogany console table that Cara recognized as being of the late Georgian period. An antique inkstand and writing case denoted the table's function as a desk. A pair of Hepplewhite mahogany cabriolet armchairs were set to either side of the table and were covered in a coral-colored slubsilk. On one wall concealed behind tambour doors were the files and accoutrements of a normal office.

Then the haughty receptionist pointed the way to a

private powder room. Proudly the girl opened the
door, disclosing what Cara felt was a positively deca-
dent room. It was lined with pale green marble and
had a matching tile floor with inserts of handpainted
hexagons depicting the more exotic members of the
orchid family. The fixtures were Sherle Wagner designs, obviously made to order because the faucet
handles were in the shape of one of the flowers shown
in the floor tiles.

Stunned by the ostentatious display, Cara hardly
knew what to say.

"This is unbelievable," she finally murmured. "Is
this really supposed to be an office?"

"Oh, no, Miss . . . Mrs. Williams," the flustered
young woman said. "This room is usually used for
entertaining important clients. But Mr. Alexander decided that, since you were to be his personal assistant,
he wanted your office adjacent to his. There's even a
connecting door between the two."

"Oh, God, give me strength," whispered Cara, then
added aloud, "Well, if mine is as elaborate as this,
what on earth is Mr. Alexander's like?"

"Oh, his is all panelled in pecky cypress; it's really
the living end. When I came here they told me that the
panelling was taken from an old mansion that was
being torn down on 72nd Street," the awed girl
announced. "There's also a little kitchenette in the
closet over here," she continued, walking over to a
previously unnoticed door and opening it to point out
a two burner stove, a small sink, and an under-the-
counter refrigerator. "It used to be used for small
cocktail parties and so on," the receptionist explained.

Cara was in a state of shock. She had expected a desk in a larger office where she would be working side by side with other employees of the magazine. It was obvious to her now that despite the fact that she had been interviewed by Jake Harding, she would not be working with him at all. Her energies would be totally directed at working with Quinn. A host of doubts suddenly filled her mind. Was this job as Quinn's personal assistant actually an experimental position for potential mistresses? In spite of the fact that he had explained her job as vital to developing the new project for the publication, she felt that he intended to groom her not so much for the magazine, but for his bed.

The primary question in her mind was whether she could redirect his intentions so that she could fully develop her talents as a designer and writer.

"Well, I guess I'll be leaving you now, Mrs. Williams. You know the way if you need me. By the way, my name is Amy. Mr. Alexander asked me to tell you that he's had personnel set up some interviews this afternoon to find a secretary for you." With a quick smile and a nod of her head, Amy left the room, leaving a speechless Cara behind her.

Slowly Cara moved around the room, pausing to examine a table, an ashtray, the back of a chair. She pushed open the tambour doors to inspect the various file drawers and cubbyholes that were hidden behind them. As she moved, she was mumbling things like: "Where do they keep the writing paper? How am I supposed to find a pencil in this place? I don't even have a typewriter for myself." As she grumbled to herself, the connecting door between her office and Quinn's opened, and the publisher entered the room, his hand outstretched in a welcoming gesture.

"Good morning, Cara. I'm glad to see you here so bright and early. How do you like your new home away from home?"

Cara's eyes widened at the sound of his voice. She had forgotten how her senses responded to his magnetism. With shortened breath she turned to look at her new employer. He was dressed in an immaculately tailored charcoal gray suit with a pale gray shirt and a beautiful silk foulard tie. As he stretched out his arm to take Cara's hand, she could see the carved carnelian and gold cufflinks he wore.

"Are you ready to start work?" he asked. "Did Amy show you around the office?"

"Well, I'm rather overcome by it all," Cara returned, deciding a good offense would be the best defense. "I certainly didn't expect anything like this. It's a beautiful room, but isn't it a little inadequate for a working designer?"

Quinn's eyebrows rose in surprise. "Just what do you mean by that?"

"Well, this is all very lovely for someone who's entertaining clients or conducting interviews or working at a more social kind of job," she said. "But I thought you wanted me to design, which involves drawing and writing. There's no drawing board, there's no tilt-top desk, there's no moveable stool— none of the things I'm going to need. And what can I do with a desk without drawers?" She was determined to keep the sophisticated man off balance. If she accepted this drawing room type of office instead of the work room she really needed, she would be acceding to his wishes right from the beginning.

She felt that she needed leverage in any relationship that might develop between them and acceptance of his plans without question could put her at a disadvantage. There was no doubt in her mind that she had caught him off guard with her criticism of what he had decided would be the perfect office milieu for his designer-playmate. Her satisfaction at the success of her attack brought a smile of triumph to her lips which in turn elicited a grin from Quinn that said "Mark one up for you!"

He strolled over to the couch and seated himself on the soft, down-filled cushion. Leaning back against the comfortable backrest, he raised his hands and locked them behind his head. Then he lifted his feet to rest them on the elegant cocktail table.

"Good lord, you can't treat good furniture like that, take your feet off the table!" Cara said indignantly.

Quinn let out a hearty laugh. "You sound just like my grandmother when you say that. She never could convince me that low tables weren't the place for feet to rest on." He straightened up from his relaxed posture and removed his feet from the table. "Since I don't want to argue with you so early in our relationship, I'll agree that you do have a point. Sit down, it's a strain on my neck to keep looking up and we have a few things to talk over before you get started."

He had indicated the seat beside him on the couch but Cara very pointedly seated herself on the high wing back chair instead.

"Do you want me to take notes?" she asked, trying to keep her voice from quivering. Her knees had started to tremble when he first opened the door to her office and the trembling hadn't stopped. If anything, it seemed to have spread throughout her body. The palms of her hands were damp and the pit of her stomach felt queasy.

Oh, he is a handsome devil, Cara thought to herself. Am I really going to be able to hold him off, or am I being foolish to even think about it? I wonder if he realizes the effect that he's having on me. Or is he so used to having every woman respond to him that it's just a game to him? Damn him . . . if he thought for one minute that I remembered that night, I think I'd wind up in his bed in no time! And it's going to be a problem to keep up the deception, because I may just want to wind up in his bed!

With one part of her mind Cara kept up a running commentary on the interaction between her and Quinn. With another part she was listening to and evaluating the directions he was giving her.

"You're right. I never gave it a thought, but you do need a good drafting table. You can call down to supply and have them order one for you. You'll probably want one of the Beylerian tables for your art supplies and . . . let's see . . . do you want to go to Charrette to choose your own materials or do you want to order through our purchasing agent?"

"Oh, I'd much rather go myself. There's nothing I like better than being turned loose in an art supply shop, unless it's being set free in a hardware store!"

"A hardware store? I might have thought you would have said jewelry store, but *hardware?*"

"Of course, all those wonderful, useful things like

bolts and drills and buzz saws and jig saws and files and . . ." The enthusiasm in Cara's voice was unmistakable.

"If you say so, but I still think a jewelry store would be more your thing." A hint of disbelief was strong in Quinn's voice.

"That was uncalled for," Cara snapped. "You really have a low opinion of me . . . or is it all women?"

"Of course not. It's just been my experience that women prefer faceted stones set in gold or platinum to hammers, jig saws and screwdrivers. But then, of course, there's always the exception to the rule . . . which you may prove to be."

Cara looked down at her nails, examining them minutely. "Yes, I think you'll find that I *am* the exception to the rule." She risked peering at the face of her employer and found his quizzical look too unsettling to maintain her glance.

Abruptly Quinn stood up. He moved from behind the round table and walked to the window, standing there, looking out on the scene below. "I won't be in the office for most of this week," he told Cara. "I'm going out to Chicago on business. You can use the time to familiarize yourself with our routine and publishing schedule. When I get back I'll be taking you around to meet some of the people involved with the production of the articles. I want you to feel fully at home before we go to Ithaca. That way you'll be able to devote yourself to creating exactly the look we want to present there. But then, I don't have to tell you what your job involves, do I?"

"You did the hiring, so you must think I know what I am doing." Cara wished she could take back her words even as she said them. She had agonized over Quinn's double entendres during her first interview, but the words she had just spoken were even more open to misunderstanding. Ignoring her own weakness, she continued as though she had said nothing out of the ordinary: "If you don't mind, I'd like to get my office set up more comfortably for my work habits, then I'd like to meet some of the people around here and do some preliminary sketches. Do you know the Laketons well enough to know whether they like contemporary art forms like weaving, pottery and woodworking?"

"As a matter of fact, they do—very much. I know that they manage to get to the Northeast Craft Fair at Rhinebeck every June and usually come away from it with work from the best exhibitors." Quinn's manner became more businesslike. "Are you thinking of incorporating their collections into the design motif?"

To Cara's relief the conversation turned to the work she would be doing. Quinn gave her some background information about his friends and tossed a few ideas at her that in turn sparked more on her part. The ensuing discussion was a precursor to numerous talks they would have during the next few weeks.

On his return from Chicago, Quinn maintained a cool, offhand manner that freed Cara of the worry that her job situation had been set up as a trap. She began to relax in the camaraderie that seemed to be developing between them—a joshing, half affectionate, half serious communication with none of the ambivalence that had been so much a part of Quinn's manner when she had first begun working with him.

Frequently they had lunch or even dinner together, usually as the inevitable continuation of a business meeting. Occasionally other members of the staff were included; sometimes, they found themselves wining and dining influential designers or manufacturers who were writing for the magazine or arranging exhibitions. Never did he hint at the night of passion they had once shared. Quinn seemed to have accepted her story about the memory lapse which had supposedly erased any recollection of their sensual encounter.

However, a week before they were scheduled to leave for Ithaca Cara's peace of mind was destroyed. She had been discussing a projected article with Quinn when she was startled by an unexpected warmth in his attitude.

"Your ideas are sound . . . and the budget gives you enough latitude to realize them." Quinn's eyes were more than approving as he spoke. "In fact, I don't think you'll have to worry about money at all." As he finished speaking, he walked over to Cara, who was standing in front of her desk, picking up sketches to illustrate her remarks. Before she could protest his move, he put his arm around her shoulder and pulled her against him. "I knew we would work well together. I like your style and I'm impressed by your ideas." He leaned down to catch her unwary mouth in a quick, hard kiss. "Unfortunately, much as I'd like to explore *all* your ideas, it's business before pleasure. I'll see you Thursday or Friday." With that as an exit line, he departed, leaving a suddenly weakened and breathless Cara behind him. His effect on her was stronger than ever.

Impossible . . . immm-possible. There's no way that I can do it . . . not if he pulls that kind of stunt on me. I'll be a wreck before long, trying to keep ahead of him. No way. Cara mused as she collapsed into one of the armchairs. I was beginning to hope . . . but there's only one kind of game that man is playing and I'm not going to play it with him. The question is, can I continue to work for him and keep it platonic? I'm an idiot to even try . . . but what if I'm wrong? Maybe he was just being friendly. After all, he does get affectionate with some of the other women. He kisses them hello and goodbye. We *have* been working hard, and he likes this new idea of mine. Don't be stupid! She scolded herself. He'll have you tied up in knots before you can count one, two, three. What am I talking about? He's got me practically tied up in knots already!

Cara sat motionless for a moment and then with a determined look about her mouth she straightened her back. Was she a woman or a mouse? So what if he was the sexiest thing around and she wanted to throw herself into his arms every time he smiled at her? Even if her skin did prickle at the memory of his strong, tender hands touching her body—so what?

"As long as I can do what Norma suggested," she whispered to herself, "as long as I can recognize my need for him and admit it without fear or shame, I can control it. I hope!"

Abruptly the door to her office opened once more and the man who was so much in her thoughts stuck his head in. "I forgot to tell you—Plan on dinner Friday night—'bye."

The door had already closed behind him before Cara could respond to his command. Somehow she got the feeling that this dinner was going to be more difficult to digest than the others she'd shared with her employer.

5

~~~~~~~~~~~~~~~~~~

"Jenny, I absolutely love this job. You know, I think I'm going to enjoy working at *Domestic Design,* after all." Cara was standing in front of the bathroom mirror combing her hair as she spoke to Jenny, who stood in the doorway watching her. "Of course I may change my mind when my boss and I are on the road. He hasn't tried anything yet, so I've been able to relax and concentrate on my work."

"I don't know why you're so down on the guy, Cara." Jenny's forehead wrinkled in thought. "He's just about the most fascinating man around. Working for him would be a dream come true."

"I find him very intimidating. He seems to think he knows so much about women." She was carefully brushing dark mascara on her lashes. "You've seen all those pictures in the society section. He's never with the same woman twice. And sometimes he looks like the cat that swallowed the canary!"

"Listen kid, sometimes me thinks thou doth protest too much." A wise little smile crossed Jenny's lips. "Didn't I tell you that going to the Halloween dance might turn out to be a good thing for you? Who knew you'd wind up working for Quinn Alexander?"

"You certainly called that one, Jen." Cara finally looked at Jenny, wondering what her roommate would think if she knew the whole story. She would probably have applauded, she was so sure that everything revolved around sex or the lack of it. Despite Cara's own misgivings about working with Quinn, she appreciated the artistic freedom she was being allowed and the challenge the job offered her creative abilities.

"Do you want breakfast before you leave for work?" Jenny's question brought Cara back to the present. "You should have something. I swear I think you're losing weight."

"I'm not losing weight, Jen, so stop mothering me. I'll grab something on the way to the office." Cara brushed past Jenny as she headed for the bedroom. "What did I do with my bag?" She began to move blankets, pillows and sheets in her search for the missing handbag.

"Here it is. Right where you left it on the chair. Honestly, Cara, you were always the organized one. What's happened to you?"

"Nothing . . . nothing really. I'm just not used to going to work like this. It's getting late, Jenny, I've got to rush."

"Will you be home for dinner tonight? Rick'll be here."

"Uh-h no, I'm having dinner out."

"You are? With whom?" Jenny was delighted.

"Oh, with someone from the office."

"Who?"

"Just someone I met." Her tone of voice was exceedingly casual.

"Getting information from you is like pulling teeth. Who is the someone? Male or female?"

"Jenny! Get off my back!"

"I'm not on your back, Cara, but what's the big secret?" Sugar couldn't have been sweeter than Jenny's voice.

"Well, if you must know, I'm going out to dinner with Quinn."

"Again? That must be the eighth time this month. But why so standoffish about telling me? Don't I tell you everything?" Jenny let a hurt tone enter her voice.

"Oh, Jenny, you know I'm not being standoffish. It's just that I didn't want you to misinterpret the whole thing," Cara said as she put on her hat. "You know it's always business and tonight's no different. We're leaving for upstate New York on Sunday. Quinn knows the Laketons well and wants to fill me in on them. If you want to know the truth, I'd rather not be going out with him." Liar, she told herself. You're frightened but you wouldn't rather be anyplace else. "It's simply a business engagement, that's all."

Jenny decided to ignore everything but the essentials. "What are you going to wear?"

"What do you mean, what am I going to wear? What I have on, of course. We're probably going straight from the office."

"So . . . that doesn't mean you can't change. From what you've told me your office is practically a home away from home. You could easily freshen up and change there. Don't you think you owe it to yourself to look your best?"

"What's wrong with what I have on?" Indignantly Cara opened her coat to display the green pleated wool skirt and pale green blouse she wore. "We're not going to the Waldorf, for goodness sake."

"You look as though you're going to the Automat . . . or someplace like it." Jenny spoke as though to a recalcitrant child. "Honestly, Cara, you can't go out with someone like Quinn looking like that, especially not on a Friday night. He'll probably want to go to one of the really fancy restaurants and you'll feel out of place if you wear that . . . all the women there will be dressed up and you'll look all wrong. You'll be miserable."

"Don't be silly, Jenny. I don't want to talk about it any more. Now you know why I didn't want to tell you with who—whom I was going out. I knew you'd start in like a mother hen. If I hadn't listened to you about going to that stupid dance I wouldn't be having these problems now."

"Cara, I'm sorry if I've upset you. Just go ahead and do whatever you want." Jenny flounced away.

"I will." Cara turned to open the door then turned back. "Jenny, I'm sorry. Please don't be angry. It's just that that man turns me upside down and I don't know what to do about it." She ran through the hall into the bedroom. "Please, Jenny, be friends?"

A brightly smiling face turned to her. "On one condition."

Knowing what was coming, Cara sighed. "What's the condition?"

"Take a change of clothes with you and make sure you look your best. You'll feel better, I promise."

"You're a wicked woman, Jenny. I don't know why I love you. All right, I give up. Help me pack my makeup and things." Cara surrendered, as she usually did in a confrontation with her roommate. In this instance she knew Jenny was right. She would feel better if she dressed up, like a soldier girded for battle.

With Jenny's help, the tan leather overnight case was quickly packed. In addition to her makeup, washcloth and soap, Cara included a wispy midnight blue Qiana dress that magically turned into *haute couture* on her well-shaped body. Narrow strapped shoes and extra sheer pantyhose with a metallic sheen joined the dress before the case was locked.

"Have fun," carolled Jenny as Cara walked out the door. "I'll expect you when I see you!"

By two that afternoon Cara was a bundle of nerves. Except for a message relayed by her new secretary, she had not heard from Quinn. She had dashed over to the nearest Sam Flax store and bought two more portfolio cases to carry the various samples and supplies she would be taking with her to the Laketons. She then rearranged her office to accommodate her tilt-top desk and wheeled stool. The elegant console table with its useless inkstand had been removed to make room for more functional pieces of furniture. She had kept the seating arrangement, enjoying its elegance.

As she sat working up some of her ideas for the Laketons, Cara suddenly realized that she had made a date for that evening with Robert before she had agreed to join Quinn for dinner. She had forgotten all about it. In fact, she'd forgotten all about Robert in the excitement of starting her new job. Idiot, she castigated herself, how could you have been so unthinking? Damn, I don't even have to be with Quinn to blot out everyone else.

Quickly she put through a call, hoping to catch Robert before he left the school for the weekend.

When she heard Robert's voice, she breathed a sigh of relief.

"Oh, it's Cara," she announced. "I'm so glad I caught you before you went home." The words tumbled out. "I forgot to tell you, Robert, I can't meet you tonight. I . . . I . . . have to work late."

"On a Friday night?"

"Well actually, I'm having dinner with Mr. Alexander. We have to discuss the presentation we'll be making this coming week." Cara's voice was apologetic. "I'm really sorry, Bob, I'd much rather go out with you. It's just that this is all so new and . . ." She was unaware that the door to the adjoining office had opened and that her employer was standing there listening to her conversation.

"We really haven't had a chance to talk much in the last couple of weeks." Disappointment was evident in Robert Avery's reply. "I never thanked you for the funny card you sent announcing your new job. I would have preferred a call, but I guess you've been very busy."

"Oh, Bob, I'm sorry. Everything seemed to happen so quickly that I didn't have a minute to call. And then I went to visit my aunt up in Maine."

"I didn't know you were going up there."

"I only decided at the last minute. It's all so complicated . . ." Cara became aware of Quinn's presence in the doorway. "Listen, I'll call you as soon as I get back from upstate New York. We have to get together to talk."

"Before you hang up, have you given any thought to the Houghton job? You promised me that you would do the renderings for me. Will you be keeping your promise?"

"Of course, I'll do the drawings as soon as I get back. We'll talk about colors and window treatment. In fact, why don't you come over for dinner on the fifteenth? We'll be back by then." She refused to hide her friendship with Robert from Quinn. In fact, she'd rather he think there was someone in her life; perhaps he would leave her alone. "I'll see you then. 'Bye now." After waiting for Robert's farewell, she carefully hung up the phone and turned to the lounging figure standing behind her. "Eavesdropping, Mr. Alexander?"

"Hardly, Mrs. Williams. I knocked, but obviously you were too involved to hear me." He moved away from the wall to come and stand next to her. "Are you working two jobs these days, Mrs. Williams?"

The curious breathlessness that seemed to be her normal response to Quinn's presence dissipated. It was replaced by a rush of anger. "Certainly not," she snapped.

"I'm glad to hear that," he returned smoothly, "because you were hired on an exclusive basis. I'm sure you realize that a great deal of money is being spent to familiarize our readers with your name, and the exclusivity of your designing talents. I wouldn't want you using those talents for the benefit of outside clients."

"But this is a prior commitment. You don't object to my completing it, do you?" Cara removed herself from Quinn's side to the safer shelter of her favorite chair. "The job is half done and Robert would have a hard time finding someone else to do the renderings now. Beside, my name has never gone on any of the work. The Houghtons have never even heard of me."

"You mean you've let Avery use your ideas without giving you any of the credit? Wasn't that foolish?" A black eyebrow went up. "Or are you so much in love that you can refuse him nothing?"

Cara's temper flared. "Since when does a job entitle an employer to meddle in the private lives of his employees? My personal relationships are none of your business. Besides, Robert wanted to credit my ideas but I wouldn't let him."

Quinn's little smile of disbelief was enough to stop her tirade and she decided it best to let the matter drop.

"What time do you want to leave on Sunday?" she asked instead.

"Changing the subject, coward? Okay, we won't pursue it further. Let's see, what time would be best for you?" He sauntered to the couch and stretched out, resting his head on his clasped hands after unbuttoning his jacket. "When do you get out of bed? Are you an early or late riser?"

Coming from Quinn, any reference to bed sent a wave of red through the clear skin of Cara's neck and face. His words brought to mind the early morning departure she had made from his apartment. Abruptly she rose from her seat to turn her back to him. "I can get up at any time that's convenient—just tell me when."

"I'd just as soon leave early. We can have breakfast before we leave the city and be on our way by nine-thirty or ten. I'll ring your doorbell at eight-thirty. Can you be ready?" His eyes were closed as he spoke.

"Of course. What about tonight?" She had turned back to face him.

"I'll talk to you about this evening in a few minutes, but before that I've got an important long-distance phone call to make. I'll be back shortly." He rose from the couch and exited the room in several easy strides.

Sinking back down in her chair, Cara allowed herself to gaze after him as he closed the door between her office and his. If only he weren't so devastatingly handsome! As though she had memorized his features, she conjured up an image of the broad forehead, jutting nose and square chin. Now she let her thoughts wander to the wide mouth with its sensuously full lower lip, remembering the feeling of its pressure on her skin. She felt a warmth in her body; a weakness invaded her legs as memories, repressed for weeks, began to freshen in her mind. She shut her eyes to close out the intoxication of his image; it would be impossible to work with him if she allowed herself to feel like this.

Allowed herself, that was funny, Cara thought, What do I do to stop myself? If I thought for one minute that he was anything but a playboy . . . but what's the use of wishing? I must get used to his seductive techniques because I'm sure to see them at work with others as well as myself. I guess he can't help it any more than he can help breathing. But he should have some discipline. He doesn't have to try to seduce *every* woman in reach. Her thoughts going around in circles, she found herself too bewildered and tired to come to any conclusion.

Before long, Cara had slipped off her shoes and curled her legs under her, resting her head against the upholstered wing of the chair. Even as she tried to resolve her ambiguous feelings, her eyelids lowered and she drifted into unconsciousness.

The silence was broken finally by the sound of the connecting door opening once again. Cautiously Quinn let it close with a soft click behind him. His softened gaze took in the slumped, slumbering form in the tapestry covered chair and paused to enjoy the look of fragility created by Cara's slender body and pale complexion. To look at her now one would never guess at what passion she was capable . . . passion he was impatient to evoke once again.

Quietly he crossed the carpeted area to the wing back chair. Stopping beside the sleeping figure, he bent over and kissed her lips. It was intended as a delicate salute to her beauty, but when, still caught in her dream, she began to respond, the kiss deepened. At the pressure of his mouth, her lips parted, accepting the exploration of his tongue. He touched her lips and then her tongue with his, extending it into her mouth, reaching for the sweet softness to be found there. Still dazed with sleep, Cara lifted her arms, placing them around his neck as he sank to his knees, enfolding her in his grasp. A soft moan came from Cara's throat as she pressed herself closer to Quinn.

Suddenly, her eyes flew open and the hands that had been fondling his head began to push at his shoulders. Immediately he lifted his mouth from hers, his breathing deepened, hers ragged.

"What . . . what are you doing?" Cara's voice trembled.

"Just acting out the story of *Sleeping Beauty*." Pushing himself back from the chair, Quinn stood up, letting a gentle hand brush Cara's tousled hair away from her face. "What better way to wake a princess from a nap than with a kiss?"

"I don't . . . don't want you to kiss me. That's not what I'm here for." Cara's slowly growing anger was like a protective cloak around her. "If you're going to take advantage of me every time I shut my eyes I'll . . ."

"Sometime I'll try to catch you with your eyes open!" A throaty laugh accompanied Quinn's outrageous answer.

"Oh-h, you're impossible!"

"Come on now, Cara, pretty girl, it's too nice a day to be angry. I'm sorry if you feel I overstepped . . . Now, where would you like to go for dinner?" The deep voice cajoled as the velvet black eyes challenged.

Cara noticed that the apology was not for the kiss, but for her interpretation of Quinn's behavior, but she couldn't help responding to his playfulness. As she answered his question, her good sense warned that she was making a mistake.

"I don't know. Where would you like to go?"

"If I told you, you'd be even angrier." Cara raised a threatening hand only to hear Quinn say, "No, no, don't hit me, I'll be good. Promise! How about someplace very de luxe for dinner?"

"Isn't it a little early for that?"

"We can start with cocktails at the Roundabout, then we'll go to Lutece or Sign of the Dove for dinner, then on to Xenon for dessert and dancing and we'll drop into Elaine's for a nightcap. How does that sound to you?"

"It sounds like a full night. Let's take it one place at a time." Once more in charge of her breathing, Cara returned to the cool, offhand manner she had tried to maintain when dealing with Quinn. "Now, if you will give me a little privacy, I would like to change."

"Do you need any help?" The sophisticated Mr. Alexander was behaving more like a high school junior than the man-about-town that he was.

"Out!" laughed the redhead. "Or the date is off!"

"Okay, okay. Don't take too long," he called over his shoulder as he walked out of the room.

Cara, you're crazy. Once more Cara was having a silent conversation with herself. You're going to get yourself in so deep you won't be able to dig your way out. That man is not interested in permanent relationships. Call a halt tonight, or else you'll find *him* calling a halt after you've lost the fight. She stepped into the green marble bathroom and began to undress. Maybe I should develop a headache before dinner. A slender white arm reached out to take the blue Qiana dress out of her overnight case. Or maybe I should get a stomach virus between now and the minute we walk out of the building. She pulled the dress over her head and picked up her hair brush, knowing full well she would do nothing to circumvent Quinn's plans for the evening.

6

~~~~~~~~~~~~~~

Softly, Cara took the coffee can out of the refrigerator and put it on the counter next to the coffee maker. With weary hands she opened the container, measured out the proper amount of coffee into the filter and then replaced the container in the machine. She poured water into the top and pushed the "on" switch; keeping her movements quiet. She had no wish to face the questions Jenny would probably greet her with this morning. How could she explain that the whole evening with Quinn had been a fiasco?

It had started pleasantly enough. The Roundabout was a charming little lounge with a talented pianist. She had looked her best after freshening up and changing; the gleam in Quinn's eyes when she walked into his office revealed that he found her unusually attractive. At the Roundabout his manner had been all she could ask for in an escort: attentive, flattering, even affectionate without being overbearing. Then, unfortunately, they had continued on to Lutece for dinner.

No sooner had they entered the quietly elegant restaurant than Quinn was spotted by a business acquaintance who insisted on treating them to drinks. By stretching one glass of white wine for an hour, Cara had managed to look as though she was participating in the jolly time everyone else seemed to be having. By then it was well past the dinner hour and she was starving. Quinn sensed her plight, bade farewell to his friend and conducted Cara into the impressive dining room where they were quickly shown to a corner table. Breathing a sigh of relief, he began to apologize for the delay, telling Cara that he had planned to expend his energy on her alone. He was not yet finished with his apology when a voice with a most intriguing accent interrupted him. "Quinn, dahling, where have you been?" The owner of the voice, Contessa Maria da Villa Ruhia, about fortyish, was small, delicate, blonde, sexy and obviously intimately acquainted with Quinn Alexander.

The Contessa invited herself to their table and joined them for dinner. Explaining that Mr. Alexander and she "had old memories to renew," she attempted to dismiss Cara. Despite Quinn's objection, his newest employee lifted her chin, and charmingly replied that she understood how "the older one was, the more important the past must be." When her escort had flashed warning signals at her with his dark eyes, and the Contessa cast a freezing glance her way, Cara was convinced that a quick retreat was in order. Before

Quinn could stop her, she was out of the restaurant, flagging a cab to take her home.

The coffee perked rhythmic accompaniment to her thoughts as Cara sat at the small round table, her chin resting on her folded hands. If there were only some way that she could get out of the visit to the Laketons, but she could think of no acceptable excuse. A letter of resignation was out of the question because of her contract and even if it were acceptable, she wasn't sure she wished to take such a drastic step.

The coffee aroma brought Jenny into the kitchen, her nose sniffing hopefully. "I'm starved. Did you make any toast to go with the coffee?"

"No."

"Do you want any? I'm going to put in an English muffin." The pajama clad figure moved sleepily around the small kitchen.

"No."

"Are you still asleep? I've seen you looking happier after stubbing your toe on a brick." Jenny leaned over to look into Cara's dejected face. "What's the matter, sweetie? I thought you'd be riding high after your dinner date last night."

"It was a business date, Jenny, not a social one. And if you must know, it was a disaster." Cara accepted a mug full of coffee from her roommate. "It started out all right, but rapidly went from bad to worse."

"How is that possible? I can't believe that *any* time spent with that gorgeous hunk of man could be bad. Did you have a fight?" Without waiting for an answer, Jenny began to scold Cara. "That's just like you, Cara. You're so on the defensive that you can't control your temper."

"You've got some nerve, Jenny. I thought you would be on my side and you can't even wait to hear my story before telling me what I've done wrong. For your information, I didn't lose my temper. In fact I was more than polite, I was Amy Vanderbilt herself!" The green eyes flashed as Cara remembered her high hopes for the evening and her disappointment at the outcome. "The trouble is that Mr. Alexander knows too many people, and some of them are very sexy blondes!"

"You mean you had competition?"

"You could say that." The two women drank their coffee in silence for a few minutes before Cara continued. "I really don't know how all this nonsense started anyway. I'm not interested in him in a romantic way; I'd be insane if I were. He's not interested in a serious relationship. He's like the sailor with a girl in every port. And I don't want to be one of them."

"I don't know how you can be so sure. Just because he's not married. After all, he did get married once, maybe he's still feeling the pain from his first experience." Jenny couldn't keep a note of compassion from her voice. "You know the saying, 'once burnt, twice shy.'"

"You wouldn't say that if you had seen that Contessa wrap herself around him last night. And I'm supposed to work with that woman." Cara stood up and walked away from the table. "It's ridiculous, I knew I should never have taken the job. I thought that I'd have no trouble controlling my feelings, but it's worse than I thought."

"What *are* you talking about?"

Suddenly Cara realized how close she had come to

betraying herself to Jenny. "Oh . . . well . . . it's so difficult working with him. You know I never expected to be his assistant. I thought I'd just be one of the crowd. So when he wanted me to go out to dinners and lunches with him I got upset. And then to have that woman making all sorts of catty remarks—She actually implied that I had taken this job in order to get the great man into my bed. She should know it was just the reverse."

"Cara! Do you mean what you just said?" Wide blue eyes sparkled. "Is that why he hired you?"

Cara groaned. "Oh please, Jenny, forget I said that. I was just being a witch. As far as I know I was hired because I'm a designer and I have a flair for writing. If there were any other reasons in Mr. Alexander's mind, I was not informed of them. Listen, can't we change the subject? I have to figure out what clothes to take with me on this trip. Quinn's picking me up tomorrow morning and I have to get a cross-country ski outfit."

"Oh great, they're having a sale at Alexander's on designer jackets and the discount place on 27th street has the best looking après ski outfit in the window."

As Jenny burbled happily about a subject close to her heart, Cara's thoughts chased through a maze of confusion. Her association with Quinn might cost her more emotionally than she had counted on or wished to pay. She had been working for him less than a month, and his impact on her was enormous. Each time she was with him it became more difficult to forget the searing passion of his embrace. The memory of their one night together should have dulled with the passing of time; instead, it became more and more vivid. The sight of his hands brought back the feeling of his fingers touching her sensitive body. The sight of his mouth speaking reminded her of the movement of his lips on hers.

"Cara, if you sit there dreaming, we'll never get to the stores." Jenny's voice once again called her to the present.

"Okay, I'll get dressed and we'll go." Cara looked at the other woman apologetically. "Sorry, there's something on my mind. I'll just be a minute."

The two women occupied themselves with trying on ski pants, boots, down jackets, gaily striped knit hats and fuzzy mittens as they went from one shop to another. In the course of their meandering through the stores, Cara decided that breakfast *à trois* the following morning would be an easier beginning for the Sunday trip with Quinn. She consulted Jenny and together they stopped at the delicacy department at Bloomingdale's to stock up on smoked salmon, cream cheese and bagels.

The next morning promptly at nine the doorbell rang announcing Quinn's arrival. Cara had spent the preceding evening choosing clothes and packing for the week's stay in upstate New York. She didn't know if she was pleased or sorry to be spending so much time in Quinn's company. Her ambivalent feelings prompted her to call her Aunt Norma for some good down-to-earth advice. She had been told that only she could decide the path she was to take. It was not up to Norma or anyone else to guide her footsteps. It was up to Cara to decide whether she was to hang onto the safety of her insulated, uninvolved way of life, using the bland relationships, such as she had with Robert Avery, as her safety line; or whether she wanted to dip her toes into the swift currents of life, taking a chance at success or failure.

"Hey Cara, I'm up to my elbows in cream cheese," Jenny called from the kitchen when the doorbell rang. "Would you answer the door, please?"

Not yet prepared to face the sardonic expression she had come to expect on the handsome dark-eyed face, Cara reluctantly opened the door.

Without waiting to be invited in, Quinn moved through the doorway and deposited a quick kiss on Cara's mouth as he walked past her.

"Good morning. I thought you'd have your coat on and be all ready to leave."

Reeling slightly from the unexpected impact of his lips, Cara mutely gestured to the already set table.

"Jenny and I thought it would be easier if we had breakfast here instead of eating on the road. Since we don't know what the weather is going to be like and you may want to stop for another . . ." She couldn't seem to stop babbling.

"This is great—I wanted a chance to say hello to Jenny again." Agreeably, Quinn slipped out of his fleece-lined jacket as he spoke.

"Everything's ready, people," Jenny said as she walked into the room carrying the coffee pot. "I'll just get the cream cheese and then we can sit down. Hi, Quinn. It's good to see you again." A quick laugh lit up the blue eyes. "You look rather dashing, if you don't mind my saying so!"

Quinn ducked his head in acknowledgment of the compliment. "I was hoping to make a good impression. How about it, Cara? Do you approve also?"

Green eyes studied the tall figure dressed in hip-hugging jeans and a white wool cable-knit turtleneck sweater. He was undeniably attractive, too much so for Cara's peace of mind. Black eyes and green eyes clashed: black challenging, green refusing. Breathing became a conscious effort for Cara as she responded to his electricity.

Exerting herself to the utmost, Cara finally broke the spell that Quinn had spun over her. If this magic was a prelude of what was to come, she would have to be superhuman in her attempt to escape his spell, if it weren't already too late. Norma had told her to allow herself to feel again, but would the consequences be worth it? She wasn't sure that she could handle a short-term romance; she had never been the type to go from man to man. She knew, from her experience with Donny, that once she made a commitment, she followed through.

"Do you want juice, Cara? Cara, hey, wake up." Jenny tapped her on the shoulder, calling her back from her discussion with herself. "If you and Quinn want to get going, you'd better start eating."

The clear pale sunshine of early March accentuated the hint of yellow on the willows growing along the distant stream. Traffic was light on Route 17 as Quinn's Rolls Corniche approached the long winding curve that led through the Ramapo foothills. After the leisurely breakfast with Jenny, Quinn and Cara had finally left the Greenwich Village appartment at half past ten and now, two and a half hours later they were approaching the Liberty area.

"I thought we'd stop for a break in about half an

hour. There's a Japanese country inn off the road not too far from Liberty. Is that okay with you?" Quinn's tone of voice suggested that he had already made up his mind and expected no objections. At Cara's vague "Mmm" of acquiescence, Quinn reached across the stick shift for her hand. Carefully he brought it up to his mouth and gently placed a kiss in the palm, holding it to his lips for a moment.

A piercing shock ran through Cara's body at his touch. She pulled her hand away, trying to disguise the force of her reaction by pointing to a large roadsign advertising the distance to Binghamton.

After the fiasco of Friday evening's dinner date, she'd be damned if she'd let him start making advances. She was *not* going to wind up in bed with the man, hard as it might prove to stay away from him.

"Why don't we stop and pick up a couple of sandwiches instead? It'll take so long to have a regular meal." Cara offered hopefully.

"I think you'll enjoy this place more than eating in the car. Besides, my back gives out if I don't take a decent break every two to three hours." Quinn's eyelids didn't even flicker at the lie.

"Oh, well . . . we wouldn't want that to happen," Cara replied mildly, suspecting that he was stretching the truth a little to tip the balance in his favor. "Have you eaten there before?"

"Two or three times. I try to stop whenever I travel this way." A note of genuine enthusiasm entered his voice. "You'll like it. The building was brought over from Japan and reconstructed next to a small pond. The owners had it landscaped by a master landscape architect who has won prizes all over the world for his Japanese gardens. Part of the pleasure of the place is being able to walk through these gardens."

"It sounds lovely. I didn't realize you were interested in gardening." Cara offered Quinn an opportunity to keep talking so that she would have a chance to think about the change in his attitude toward her, a change that was becoming more obvious by the minute. The safe, noncommittal manner that he had maintained for the past weeks of their association had lulled her into thinking that she no longer had anything to fear from him. Now she wondered if that had been a false security.

Until this trip, they had encountered each other only in busy, rushed interludes. Cara had thought that they were approaching friendship, which she considered a less dangerous relationship to have with Quinn. Of course, feeling as she did about him, friendship could be an insidious association, masking the passion that existed between them with affection. And that was just the problem. Though she might claim to despise the man for what he had done, she was more than attracted to him. She was beginning to be obsessed by him. His touch a moment ago had been enough to ignite the smoldering fire within her. She would have to force a feigned indifference to that touch if she was to get through this week.

To protect herself from further contact with him, Cara moved as close to the door as the bucket seat would allow and tucked her hands beneath her arms, commenting on the chilliness of the weather.

"It's almost spring, but there's no denying that

winter is still here." Nothing safer than the weather, she told herself. "Did you get a weather report on Ithaca?"

"It's probably for snow. We should get in some good cross-country skiing up there. I hope you brought some warm clothes."

An uneasy silence descended on them and Cara said the first thing that came to mind. "How did you get started in publishing, Quinn?"

"It just happened. Why? Should I be flattered that you're exhibiting an interest in my past?"

"Don't be silly, I'm not trying to flatter you. I'm really curious. Somehow, I always think of you as the outdoor type, an interior design magazine just doesn't seem to be your metier."

"Now I'm not flattered, I'm flattened!"

"Oh, come on. If anything, I should think you'd be more interested in a sports publication or something like that."

"I might have been, except that I'm trained as an architect," Quinn replied softly. "I was interested in designing homes that were more than just split-level or ranch-style boxes. I wanted to do something special. Like most young people, I was very idealistic. Then came a sharp drop in home building and it was a case of 'last hired, first fired' at the company where I worked." He became quiet for a while.

"So what happened next?"

"I began to do some work for contractors who specialized in renovating existing buildings, then I wrote a couple of articles for one of the do-it-yourself mags. Along the way I bought out the contractor, convinced a bank to invest in me, built up the company, and bought *Domestic Design* magazine so I could preach what I like to practice—architecture."

"You make it sound so simple. It can't have been all that easy, you're still relatively young to have achieved so much." Cara turned in her seat to look at Quinn. "You must be a millionaire to be in the position you're in. That's quite an accomplishment."

"I must confess that I had an advantage over the average guy. I was born into a successful family; that gave me a good line of credit. It helped." Quinn flipped the turn indicator as he spoke. "We're almost there. Right now, I'm more interested in sushi and tempura than ancient history."

Agreeably Cara held back her questions; if Quinn didn't want to talk about his achievements, she wouldn't pursue the matter. To herself though, she murmured words of congratulations to this complex man whom she was slowly discovering. So far she had seen him as a playboy, a successful publisher and a man of the world. Now she could contemplate his prowess as an artist; closer in temperament to her world, possibly more knowable.

"Not too much further—I think it's just around the next curve."

As promised, the next bend in the road brought them in sight of a discreet weathered sign with gold lettering announcing the Inn of the Five Pines. They drove up a long winding driveway, past a thick planting of coniferous trees to a rolling meadowlike area. Nestled into one of the narrow valleys was a long, low building with an artfully shaped roofline that was distinctly Japanese. A crisply defined path of water-smoothed pebbles led from the parking lot to the broad steps that edged the front of the building. A massive wooden door with handsome brass handles marked the entrance. The garden that fronted the inn was covered with raked sand into which were set exquisitely shaped rocks and evergreen plants: some of the plants were grouped so that contrasting textures and colors enhanced each other and pleased the eye, others in solitary splendor so that the complete beauty of the shrub itself could be enjoyed. A path of round slices of tree trunks drew one down a gentle slope to a whispering stream where willows and bamboo grew. Overall there was a feeling of timelessness, of peace and tranquility that soothed the viewer.

"Oh Quinn, it's beautiful! How lovely it is just standing here. I never would have believed anything like this existed in the middle of the Catskills." Cara started to laugh. "This is wonderful . . . I wouldn't be surprised if I saw a replica of Mount Fuji on the other side of the stream."

"I knew you'd like it. Let's go inside. The food is just as impressive and the service is excellent." Casually he took her hand to lead her into the building.

Beyond the oak doors a hostess wearing a kimono waited to show them to their table. After taking their coats, she indicated the paper slippers with which they were to replace their shoes before stepping on the tatami mats in the dining room.

As Cara unzipped her wine-colored leather boots, she looked up at Quinn with a laugh. "I can't get over this. It's like being in another country."

"Well, in a sense you are. And as long as you're someplace other than your homeland, you have to follow the customs of that land, so off with the shoes and on with the slippers."

"I wonder why?"

"If you wore hard-soled shoes in the tatami room the rice straw mats would be ripped to shreds in no time. And when you have to sit with your feet under you, its more comfortable with the shoes off." A wicked grin creased his cheeks. "Need I say more?"

The hostess, who had introduced herself as Mitsouko, conducted them into the spacious tatami room where she seated them at a low lacquered table that had a pit beneath it. Smiling at this combination of traditional Japanese seating and Western comfort, Cara slid her legs under the table and allowed them to dangle into the shallow opening.

"Lucky for you," she said to Quinn. "This hole will just about hold your long legs. I can't quite see you curled up on your heels all through lunch."

"A very advanced people, the Japanese. Have you ever had Saki?"

"No, but I wouldn't mind trying some. I understand it's good for taking the chill off."

Quinn quirked an eyebrow at his companion as he ordered two bottles of Saki with an extra large portion of sushi. The hostess thanked him and left after wishing them an enjoyable meal.

Cara leaned her elbows on the table, then rested her chin on her hands. "This place is lovely . . . all those shoji screens and the pottery. And this flower arrangement . . . it's like a piece of sculpture. I never would have thought three chrysanthemums, five leaves and the tip of a pine branch could be so absolutely perfect. I'm good at flower arranging, but the simplicity of the Japanese arrangements is a little beyond my abilities."

Quinn leaned forward, matching her posture by putting his arms on the table and resting his chin on his cupped hands. "I have a feeling that you can do whatever you want to do, especially if it interests you enough."

"You're very flattering." Long darkened lashes rested against a flawless cheek. "I don't think I'd be a good politician though, or a good bookkeeper or . . ."

"I can understand bookkeeper, but why not a politician?"

"Well, if you haven't noticed, I have a pretty vile temper, and I'm not always diplomatic when I'm annoyed."

A long, well-shaped hand reached across the table to clasp Cara's wrist in a gentle, firm grip. A light tug brought her hand down to the table where Quinn clasped it in his, rubbing his thumb across her knuckles as though he were stroking satin. The eroticism of so ordinary a gesture made Cara catch her breath.

"You've never told me anything about yourself, Cara. Other than you're a widow. What were you like when you were a little girl? Where did you live and where are your parents now?"

"There's nothing spectacular about me. I was born and grew up in north Jersey, near the New York state border. My parents still live there—they own an art supply and framing shop. I think my interest in art developed because many of their friends were artists. It's an advantage to be able to talk to people in the field when you're deciding on a career."

The arrival of the waitress with the first course

interrupted Cara's words. Her attention was drawn to the oblong wooden platters on which were arranged portions of sushi—delicately flavored raw fish slices on vinegared rice accompanied by a heap of wine-soaked ginger slices. Next to each platter was a small dish of dipping sauce and a pair of chopsticks. As Cara exclaimed over the beauty of the arrangement, the waitress added two covered lacquered bowls and two small porcelain Saki bottles, along with thimble-sized saki cups.

"You'll have to tell me what's what. I've never eaten this before." Cara leaned closer to the table, examining the food and sniffing delicately at the miso soup in her bowl. "The last time I ate Japanese food, in fact the only time, I had hibachi steak . . . you know, the kind they cook right at the table. I'll never forget the chef's performance, using his knife as though it were an extension of his arm. He moved so fast the blade was a blur. What's that?" she asked, pointing to several small cylinders of rice on her platter.

"Tekkamaki. It's tuna and rice wrapped in a special seaweed. When we leave we can stop at the sushi bar and watch the chef roll them." Quinn poured some Saki into the miniscule holders. "Here, have some of this while it's still warm." He handed her a cup. "Do you know how to use the chopsticks?"

"If I can use them the same way I would in a Chinese restaurant, I do." She took the wine from him and held the cup up beside his. "Are you going to make a toast?"

"You'd better believe it. Let's see . . . here's to you and me and the success of this trip. May we each get our heart's desire." Dark, wicked eyes, full of a warmth that Cara could almost feel, held hers, exerting an invisible mastery.

With the greatest effort, Cara finally broke the hold, rushing into a series of stuttered questions about the food, and ending with a request for a demonstration of the best way to eat it.

"Okay, first you take a slice of the ginger like so." Skillfully Quinn wielded the two sticks of wood, picking up the pinkish ginger with careful precision. "Then you lay it on top of the fish like so," the demonstration continued, "and then you pick it up like so and pop it into your mouth . . . in two bites if you're experienced at it or in one large mouthful if your chopsticks begin to slide." By the end of his sentence his cheek was bulging with sushi and Cara was laughing at his nonsense.

The use of the chopsticks came back to Cara with no difficulty but, when her hand tired of gripping them, Quinn took over the job, choosing the most appetizing tidbits and placing them in her mouth. Each time he lifted something to her lips he would capture her eyes with his, letting his desire speak to her in the depth of his gaze. To distract herself, Cara would sip some miso soup from the small lacquered bowl or some Saki. The time spent over the meal, which progressed without her being aware of the service, took on a magical quality. Periods of talk in which the two exchanged bits of information about themselves became shorter as the moments of speechless communication became longer. A languor took over Cara's body in the hushed, almost empty room, a

languor similar to that which followed the act of love.
And Quinn was making love to her; without touching,
without talking, every move of his eyes over her body
was arousing her.

It was only when the waitress presented them with
the tray of hot towels and the heat touched Cara's
hands that she was reminded of her surroundings.
With a startled gasp she came back from the secret
place she had been sharing with her lover. Her cheeks
flamed red when she realized what had happened and
she pushed herself away from the table, wriggling off
the pillow in an effort to draw her feet up out of the
hollow beneath the table.

"Easy, easy, you'll get yourself all tangled up,
babe," Quinn cautioned her softly. "Here, let me help
you." Quickly he extricated himself from his position
and with strong hands, lifted her from the floor.

As he stood her upright, he turned her to face him
and let his arms slide from under her arms to her waist,
pulling her close to his body. Overcome for the
moment by the aftereffect of the Saki and the feel of
his hands on her, she wilted against him, resting her
forehead against his broad chest, feeling the beat of his
heart. She took a deep breath, inhaling the combined
odor of his aftershave and his masculinity, closing her
eyes to concentrate more fully on the sensuousness of
the experience.

"Are you all right?" Concern in his voice brought
her upright and away from the comfort of his warmth.

"I was just dizzy for a moment . . . too much sitting
and maybe a little too much wine." She attempted a
reassuring smile. A shaky hand went up to push her
hair away from her face. "I'll be better when we get

outside." She had no wish for Quinn to know how much his closeness affected her.

Gently Quinn put his arm around her waist, carefully guiding her out of the dining room to a bench in the foyer. "Here, sit down for a minute while I collect our shoes and coats. It's cooler in here so you should feel a little better." He studied her face, and as the color returned to normal he felt a rush of tenderness for her. He took her boots from the waiting hostess and, kneeling in front of Cara, lifted first one foot and then the other to slide them into the shoes. His hands gripped her ankles one at a time as he carefully pulled up the zippers, then smoothed the leather around her legs. It was such an intimate action that Cara once more felt the stab of desire. With supreme effort she rose to her feet and moved away from the man who was having such a disruptive influence on her senses.

As the hostess bowed and whispered thank you and *Sayonara*, Cara walked quickly out of the restaurant. She knew that her relationship with Quinn was about to take on a new dimension; his manner had changed from the cool, businesslike exchanges they had been indulging in since the interview, to the more personal, sexually challenging confrontation they were having today.

The constant question was whether or not she could handle an affair with him and the inevitable ending of such an affair. To her consternation, she had discovered today that the feelings he aroused in her went beyond mere desire; she was falling in love with him. The brightness of his mind, the sharpness of his wit, the tenderness of his concern, were weaving cords around her that might prove too strong to loosen. If she thought there was the slightest chance that he felt the same way about her she would have no hesitation to commit herself to him, but . . .

What would happen if she decided to take a chance on winning his love? There was no rule that said he would remain uncommitted for the rest of his life. Perhaps she could . . . but no, that was wishful thinking. She had to decide one way or the other. She would either accept an affair with this fascinating, exciting man who was rapidly dominating her every waking moment, or she would have to break away from him completely, without regard for her contract or the repercussions that would result from breaking it.

The thoughts whirled around in Cara's head as she walked to the car, unaware that she was almost running.

"Hey, slow down. There's no hurry." Quinn's voice brought her back from her concentration. "Here, what's wrong?" He caught up with her, catching her arm and swinging her about.

She stopped, held still as much by his presence as by his strength. The pale sun shone on her face as she looked up at him, highlighting strands of gold in her fiery red hair. Her eyes were a smoky green, questioning, weighing, deciding, as she examined his face minutely. Gradually they cleared to their normal bright color. She had made her decision: She would ride with the storm . . . and whatever the ending she would live with it.

7

C̶ara, we're here.". The butterfly touch of Quinn's lips against hers woke Cara from a deep sleep. For a moment she lost her bearing, forgetting where she was. She opened her eyes slowly, confused by the cramped position in which she found herself, then realized that the leather pressing against her cheek was the backrest of the seat in Quinn's car. Carefully she turned, stretching her legs out, then extending her arms until they reached the windshield.

"Oh . . . I forgot where I was." She pushed her hair back from her face, taking out the combs that held it in place. "I didn't realize there'd be a view of the lake from the house. What time is it?"

"It's almost five-thirty. You've been asleep for the last hour and a half. What company you turned out to be." Quinn pulled a wry face as he laughed at his sleepy-eyed passenger. "I should have brought along a good record player and a talking book."

"I'm sorry, Quinn, but it's your fault. I'm not used to having wine with my lunch. See what happens when you try to corrupt the incorruptable? It's trouble every time!" Cara unwound herself enough to take Quinn's hand as he reached into the car to help her out. "This is beautiful. I had no idea how beautiful! When you said an early Victorian home, you didn't mention that it was such a gem . . . all that gingerbread and that octagonal tower. Fantastic."

"Wait until you see the inside, it's even better." Strong hands lifted the suitcases from the trunk of the car, swinging them to the ground. "Where's your portfolio? I thought I put it in with the bags. Oh, here it is, it slid under the seat."

"Thank goodness. I could just see myself without my tape and pads." Cara took the large carrying case from Quinn and started to walk across the flagstone walk to the entrance of the house, exclaiming over the beauty of the location. The walkway was a thin gray ribbon between high snowbanks; the pristine snow stretching away from the house.

The yellow building, trimmed in white, faced east. The rear of the house looked out on Cayuga, the longest of the Finger Lakes, and the rolling hills of Tompkins County. The property surrounding the house was level in front, sloping steeply down to the lake in the rear. The quiet, pierced by the calls of nesting birds unknown to a New York City dweller, recalled Cara's childhood visits to Maine.

The two approached the dark red door with the large brass eagle centered above the frosted window. Just as Quinn was about to use the old-fashioned knocker, the door was opened by a rosy-cheeked woman who smiled broadly at him and stood on tiptoe to place a kiss on his cheek.

"Mr. Alexander, I thought you'd never get here. And is this the lady who's going to do all the work? My, you look as pretty as a flower . . . such beautiful hair." The words came tripping from her mouth almost too fast to hear.

"Mrs. Stevens, how's my girlfriend? Cara, this is Louisa Stevens, the Laketon's housekeeper and my secret passion." Quinn had dropped the suitcases and put his arm around the laughing woman. "The only problem is that if her husband William ever finds out we're carrying on, he's liable to shoot me, and then what would I do?"

"You surely do go on Mr. A. C'mon, Mrs. Williams, I've got your room all ready for you if you want to go up now." She moved back into the hall to allow Cara and Quinn to enter the house. "I don't have to show you where to go, do I, Mr. A.? Dinner will be ready about six-thirty. I can serve it in the dining room or in the study, whichever you prefer. You'll have to serve yourselves. William gets home for dinner at seven and I like to have it ready for him, so I'll be leaving as soon as I've fixed yours."

"Where are the Laketons, Mrs. Stevens? They're supposed to be here too." Quinn sounded surprised to learn that their hosts were absent, but Cara wondered if his surprise was real or assumed.

"They *were* here, but Mr. Laketon's father called earlier. Some kind of family emergency that had to be attended to. He said they'd call as soon as they had anything to tell you. They wanted you and Mrs. Williams to make yourselves at home and have a good time 'til they got back."

Quinn turned to Cara, a wary look on his face. "I'm very sorry this had to happen, Cara. Will it be all right with you if we stay here? We can make other arrangements if you'd like."

"Don't be silly, Quinn. I don't see any reason to change our plans unless you do." She turned to Mrs. Stevens. "I'd love to see my room, Mrs. Stevens. If I don't take off these boots and change into something else I'll think I've grown into these clothes and that they'll never separate from me. Somehow traveling always makes me feel so grubby."

"I know just what you mean. You come right along with me." Bustling along, she led Cara up the curved staircase and along the upper hallway to a spacious bedroom at the back of the house. "You'll have a good view of the lake from here, and the sun won't wake you in the morning." She whisked into the room, pulling at the bedspread, straightening a towel on the towel bar, and inspecting for any overlooked dust. "Your bathroom is through that door and this is your closet." She opened the appropriate doors displaying their contents. "I don't come in until noon, so you'll have to get breakfast for yourself and Mr. Alexander, unless you sleep late. Then I'll get it for you. There's plenty of food in the fridge, and I always leave a pitcher of pancake batter ready. I better get back to my kitchen now, else we'll have burnt offerings for dinner." She giggled at her own joke, then disappeared through the door.

Thankful to be alone, Cara surveyed the large room. The furnishings were a hodge-podge of country Victorian pieces, a mixture of oak, walnut and pine; the only worthwhile piece was a small upholstered rocker on a stationary base. It had a charm that lifted it out of the ordinary and prompted Cara to use it in her redecorating scheme. Plain white organdy tieback curtains over pull shades hung at the windows and the walls were covered with a paper printed with huge roses on a white background. The shape of the roofline created a perfect bay window in which Cara could visualize a deep window seat with an upholstered cushion on it. At present, it held only an old-fashioned radiator.

The double bed, with its high veneer headboard and low footboard, was covered with a white candlewick spread. The aged mattress had a discernible dip in it, giving an indication of the difficulty Cara would have moving around on the bed.

After examining her surroundings, Cara opened her duffle bag and began to empty it. She quickly hung up her things in the closet and put her underwear and pantyhose away in the drawers of the marbletop dresser. She had included two caftans for use in the evenings, preferring the loose lounge robes for the easy comfort they offered. Now she left one out to wear for dinner.

Debating with herself whether to take a fast shower followed by a short nap or a long soak and no nap, she was interrupted by a quick tapping on the bedroom door.

She called out, bidding whoever it was to come in, then was startled to see Quinn. "Hi, I'm just getting my things put away. Is there something you want?"

"Only to make sure everything is okay. I told Louisa to set up dinner in the study before she leaves. The dining room is too large for just the two of us." He walked over to the window to stand looking out at the scene. "We'll go for a walk tomorrow. There are some lovely trails along the lakefront. Would you like that?"

"Of course, but I thought we came here to work."

"You will . . . there's plenty of time for work." He finally turned to Cara, then walked over to take her hands as he looked into her face and said: "I want you to know, Cara, I didn't set this up. Ted and Judy were supposed to be here. I wouldn't do this to you."

Masking her surprise at his open acknowledgment that she might be concerned, and recognizing that she might have reason to be, she answered in a level voice. "I know. I didn't think you'd drive for five and a half hours just to seduce me, Quinn."

He grinned in appreciation of her directness. "You know that I'm tempted, don't you?"

"I . . . really haven't given it too much thought." Lowered lids screened the flare of desire in her eyes.

"Liar!" A soft kiss touched each eyelid, then he moved away and Cara knew the moment of danger was past.

A flare of heat began deep within her and worked its way through her body, bringing a fine beading of perspiration to her face. She was aware of the flush that accompanied it, turned to the mirror and picked up a powder puff to mask her weakness.

"If you're through playing, I'd like to take a nap.

116

What time shall I meet you downstairs?" She kept her eyes on the mirror, refusing to meet his glance.

"In about an hour or so . . . unless you're so hungry you want to make it sooner."

"No, that's fine." She wished he would leave the room. "Well, if that's all . . ." She drifted to the door, holding it ajar for him to leave.

He paused on his way out, placing a hand on her shoulder, allowing it to slide down to her wrist, then gently pulled her to him. They moved as in slow motion, unaware of the inevitability of their actions. Gently, carefully, he leaned forward while their bodies were still apart, and placed his lips on her upraised mouth. They stood, the only points of contact the two pairs of hands and their mouths, asking and answering, probing and promising. It was a compact announcing their intentions without wishing to rush the next part of their engagement.

Still moving slowly, Quinn lifted his head. Then he touched Cara's lips with the tip of his finger, a serious look on his face as though he were seeing her for the first time. She said nothing, made no move, gave no response other than her kiss. Finally he continued out of the room, releasing her hand, finger by finger, as though unwilling to break contact with her. She stood silent as the door closed behind him, then touched her lips to verify the memory of his wordless communication.

Drained by the event, Cara picked up her hairbrush and began to stroke it through her shoulder length tresses. As she performed the mechanical action, she tried to understand what had just taken place between herself and Quinn. If she didn't know his reputation, she would have said that he had made an unspoken commitment to her, but that was surely wishful thinking. The sweetness of the kiss, given without passion or domination, was beyond anything in her experience. She knew she was playing a dangerous game, but whatever the eventual cost, she also knew the immediate rewards were great. The promise of his lovemaking was a promise she could not resist.

Later she sat in scented bathwater, still pondering the potential for love that was between the two of them, knowing that she was spinning daydreams. At last she shook her head, ridding herself of dreams, and began to soap her body. She rubbed the soapy washcloth over her satin skin, and suddenly it was as though Quinn's hands were moving over her. Impatient with herself, she stood and turned on the shower, then lowered the temperature of the water to cool her thoughts.

An hour later she was dressed. She wore a caftan made of a silky fabric in a swirling, vibrant blue green. She put on a single gold chain from which was suspended a carved jade pendant that rested in the hollow between her breasts. Her hair hung loose, waving softly about her face, clinging to her cheekbones. On her face, she had used only lip gloss, a lightly applied green eyeshadow and a touch of dark mascara. Had she spent hours at a beauty salon, she could not have looked more beautiful or more desirable. The soft material of her robe clung to the roundness of her breasts, touched the curve of her hips, and outlined the length of her legs. Though it covered her completely, it revealed her body provocatively, more subtle than blatantly exposed naked skin.

She walked down the steps, trailing a hand on the banister, her eyes on her feet. She was unaware that Quinn was standing at the door to the study, his gaze riveted upon her as she moved toward him. She became aware of his presence when she reached the lower floor and looked up to see the blaze in his eyes. Quickly he turned his head, unable to look at her without acknowleging his desire. For the moment he had no wish to let her know the impact she had on him.

"Mrs. Stevens lit the fire in the fireplace before she left; it's nice and warm in here." Was there the slightest tremor in his voice?

Cara walked into the book-lined room and glanced around, taking note of the deep, comfortable old sofa covered in a flowered cretonne, the big lounge chairs and worn oriental rug thrown over the shabby carpeting. Despite the used quality of the room, it had a welcoming feeling to it. One could say a happy feeling.

"I don't know what's in that casserole, but it smells heavenly." She went to the table and lifted the lid of the pottery serving dish. "The chicken must be cooked with wine and a touch of marjoram . . ." She sniffed at the steam rising from the food. "Maybe even some garlic. I didn't realize I was so hungry. I want to dive right into this. You'd better get over here if you want any or I'll finish it before you have a chance." Nonsense, keep talking nonsense or you might say something you don't want to. "Did you take a nap? You must have been tired after that long drive. At least I slept on the way . . . I thought you would let me do some of the driving." Why doesn't he say something? God, he looks fabulous. The pale blue silk shirt against his tanned skin enticed her. *What's come over me? I feel like . . . a bride.* The words rose up from her subconscious and silenced her riotous thoughts.

Quinn pulled out a chair and pushed it against the back of Cara's legs, urging her to sit. Nervously she allowed him to move her toward the table which had been set in front of the window, then watched as he went to the chair opposite and sat down.

"This pâté is marvelous." Cara sampled the delicious appetizer, nodding her head when Quinn raised the wine bottle with a questioning look. As he poured the light Rhine wine into her glass, she began to butter her roll, unable to sit still, unable to bear the constant fluttering of her heart. "Did Mrs. Stevens make this? It's really very good. Has she been with the Laketons for very long? I know . . ."

"Cara, enough, be still, relax. The big bad wolf isn't going to get you if you stop talking." Quinn lifted the lid of the casserole. "Here, let me serve you some chicken, I think you're giddy from hunger."

"I am not . . . I . . ." Cara let her lips curve in an unwilling smile. "I guess I feel a little uncomfortable. I'm not a woman of the world and this situation is more than I had bargained for." She took a deep breath. "I feel better now. Can we start over and forget my modest maiden act?"

Black eyes lit with humor. "Well, if that's what you want, I'd be more than happy to. How shall I consider you? If not modest maid, how about muddled Mrs.?"

A chuckle answered his nonsense. "A better term I'm sure. Muddled is right. As long as it doesn't show in my work." More at ease, Cara began to eat with enjoyment. "I don't know why I let myself get into such a tangle whenever I'm faced with a new situation." She sipped her wine.

"It's not an unnatural thing to do." He gazed at the woman opposite him, a challenge in his eyes. "You acted the same way the first time you came up to the office . . . remember? I thought you'd resign before you ever started to work for me."

A tint of red touched Cara's cheeks. "That's not fair. I was in a panic. Being interviewed by the great Quinn Alexander when all I expected was an interview with Jake. And then to be offered the job as your assistant when I had hoped for nothing more than a beginning position on the staff. You can't blame me for being suspicious of the suave, debonair man who was examining me under a very large magnifying glass."

"Do you want more chicken? I don't blame you, I suppose I expected you to be somewhat more sophisticated, more experienced." He grinned at her as he covered the casserole. "Was it really such a big magnifying glass?"

"But you knew I hadn't worked before. That I had just graduated." She knew there was a hidden reference to their original meeting, but she refused to permit Quinn the satisfaction of knowing that she was completely aware of the evening of the masquerade. She felt stronger for her subterfuge.

"I wasn't really speaking of work experience," he murmured. "But let's drop the subject for now . . . it's r.ot important. This is really good, isn't it?"

The conversation lagged as they finished their meal, but their awareness of each other became more pronounced. Again and again their eyes tangled, held by a force that was fast becoming too strong to be denied. Cara's breathing became jagged and finally she was forced to stand and leave the table. As she walked past Quinn's chair, he reached out for her hand, halting her progress. His touch was electrifying, renewing the fire of her response. She was voiceless, motionless, feeling like the prey of some wild jungle beast, frozen in terror.

"Please . . ." A whisper escaped her frozen lips. "What do you want of me?" Her voice was husky as she spoke.

The grip on her wrist tightened, then shifted as Quinn stood. Before he answered he pulled her to him, taking the sweep of her red gold hair in his left hand and holding her head immobile. His darkened eyes caressed her face, resting on her slightly parted lips as though anticipating the coming moment.

"What do I want of you?" His voice was thoughtful. "Everything. Everything you have to give, Cara. Witch . . . my witch. Your green eyes bewitch me and I want you."

As he finished his sentence, he lowered his head, pressing his mouth against hers, plundering, thrusting, besieging. He was the warrior; she, his captive.

The assault on her senses took her by surprise, gave her no time to bolster her defenses against the need to respond to the invasion of her mouth. Her knees turned to water and she swayed against his chest, placing a hand on his shoulder to steady herself. When he felt the first weakening of her armor, he let go of her wrist, wrapping his arm around her waist to support her and draw her closer to his strong body. Through the thin silk of her gown she felt the muscles of his legs, the strength of his hips and the power of his desire.

Helplessly, she raised her arms, reaching around his shoulders, straining to hold him closer.

His tongue met hers in quick, rapierlike movements that soon changed to languid strokes, touching, tasting the interior of her mouth, then her lips. Moving his head, he tasted her ears, her neck, and then returned to her mouth, satiating his need.

"Oh Quinn . . . oh, don't let me go. Hold me, hold me." The words were less than a sigh.

"You're so beautiful, so sweet. I want to eat you, you taste so good," he answered in husky tones.

Still holding her mouth with his, he swung her up into his arms, moving to the deep, cushioned couch, then sinking into it, with Cara enfolded next to him. Gradually, he released her from his crushing embrace, letting his hands move over her body, stroking her back, then her sides, letting the tips of his fingers come to rest on her breasts. He could feel the reaction of the swelling nipples as they responded to his touch and thrill after thrill pierced Cara. Blindly she placed kisses on his lowered head, moaning when she felt his mouth through her dress. She arched away from the pillows, allowing his searching hand to grasp the zipper of her gown, twisting away from the clinging fabric, making it easier for him to release her from the lacy scrap of material that confined her breasts. Triumphant, his seductive lips took possession of first one pink nipple and then the other, caressing them with his skilled tongue, bringing the fire inside her to white heat.

She felt an aching emptiness within that begged to be assuaged, to be made complete. Her hands moved under his shirt, across his back, down to his waist, rapturous at the feel of his skin against her palms. She pressed against him, pulling him closer, stroking his hips, grasping his buttocks.

"Oh God, Cara! Keep touching me. I need you so . . . don't stop." He groaned as he shifted his body to position it over hers, letting her feel the full strength of his masculine form. He lifted her hips, sliding the dress from under them. Then the bikini panties were slipped off, following the blue green mass of silk onto the floor. Her flesh glimmered pearllike in the dancing light of the fireplace. Her eyes were opaque with desire, her cheeks flushed with the heat of lovemaking.

Her hands were impatient as they unbuttoned Quinn's shirt, then quickly moved down to his belt and the zipper of his slacks; her mouth was consuming as she kissed his shoulders, neck and chest, touching his flat, male nipples with her tongue, trembling in response to his tremor.

"Look at me, don't close your eyes . . . look at me." Half command, half supplication, his words were whispered with a quivering intensity.

She raised her eyelids, allowing her gaze to be captured by his, aroused even further by the eroticism of that shared look. He lowered his hands to her thighs, separating them, then stroking them as his fingers climbed to the moist core of her body, still holding her eyes with his, making the sensations more vivid with that contact. Her breath stopped then started in a series of little moans deep in her throat; her eyes widened.

"Quinn, please. Quinn . . . Please love me," she begged. She hardly heard his sounds of acquiescence as he entered her warmth, creating a whirling vortex of sensation that exploded in fragments of light and color. As she cried his name in ecstasy, he let out an unconsciously triumphant laugh, watching the fire-works in her eyes, joining her in that final explosion.

"Oh my witch, my beautiful witch," were the words Cara heard moments later as she slowly came back from the almost trancelike state that had been the aftermath of the intense emotions accompanying her joining with Quinn. Her lax arms tightened around him and her head turned to receive his kiss.

"Oh, Quinn . . ." Her voice trailed off. She didn't know how to express the joy she felt. She had never experienced such fulfillment.

"You're wonderful . . . beautiful, and I'm never going to let you go." He began to caress her once more, placing nibbling kisses along her jawline and down her neck to the erratically beating pulse there. "You . . . are . . . beyond . . . belief!"

Slowly the dance of love commenced again, with all the skill and grace that the two participants could endow it. Once again Cara's body responded to the deft touches of her lover, inspiring him in turn with her responsiveness. This time they lingered, having lost the urgency that had characterized their first, almost feverish, lovemaking; this time they relished each step, working toward their crescendo with feelings of won-der and joy, urging each other on to greater efforts with soft words of love. And once more they called out to each other from that peak of rapture that was the culmination of their desire.

They lay in each other's arms afterward, Cara brushing the thick black hair from Quinn's brow, tracing the hollows of his eyes with a loving finger,

examining the shape of his nose and the curves and
angles of his face. She felt a tenderness toward him, a
need to enfold him and care for him that went beyond
anything she had ever felt before. And then she
realized, as she gently kissed the corners of his mouth,
that she had fallen in love with this arrogant man. She
loved him as she had never loved before and in that
moment of recognition, she felt a rush of hopelessness
—he had no wish for a lasting love, he wanted only
fleeting relationships, no involvement. She would
either have to accept it or leave him before he
destroyed her.

As she watched him, his eyes closed in sleep and
she could let the tears drop. She laid her head on his
chest, feeling snug against his side on the deep couch,
and held on to the illusion of closeness for as long as
possible. Like mice on a treadmill, her thoughts raced
in her mind. Should she leave Ithaca tomorrow or
shouldn't she? Should she remain as Quinn's assistant
or shouldn't she? Should she quit her job or shouldn't
she? *Could* she leave him feeling the way she
did . . . or should she? Even as the questions whirled
around in her head, her mind refused to trouble itself
any longer and drifted off to sleep.

The only sound in the room was the crackling of the
fire in the grate, warming and shining upon the two
sleeping people entangled in each other's arms.

The flames from the fire had died down and only
the glowing embers were left in the grate. In the hall
the grandfather clock softly chimed the hour of three,
wakening Quinn. His eyes flicked open, alert and
intelligent, aware immediately of all that had hap-

pened and the woman in his arms. He tightened his grip on her, watching through half open eyes her lashes lying like soot on her cheeks, the softly curved mouth slightly parted in sleep. He lifted his hand to her face and delicately trailed a finger across her mouth and down her neck.

"Cara . . . Cara . . ." Her sleep was too deep. Carefully he moved his legs and got up off the couch. She stirred in her sleep, murmuring his name with a sigh.

A smile touched his lips as he listened to her, then he stooped to scoop her up in his arms, ignoring the scattered clothes, and moved out of the room. In her half-waking, half-sleeping state, she lifted her arms around his neck and snuggled her head into the hollow of his shoulder, making purring sounds.

Lightly, Quinn went up the staircase and into Cara's bedroom. Still hugging her to him, he reached with one hand to turn back the candlewick spread, then bracing his knees against the edge of the mattress, placed her on it. He walked around the bed to get onto it on the other side, missing the cautiously opened eye watching his movements. As he sat down, the eye closed again, hiding the gleam that shone there. With a soft exhalation of air, Quinn lay down and pulled the spread over them. Ready to sleep once again, he reached for Cara before he sank into slumber. She allowed him to cuddle her body against his and then, when he had settled down quietly, quickly rolled over, half on him, half off, and grabbed for his sides.

"What . . . what's going on?" he demanded in a startled voice.

"You're not ticklish, damn you," she laughed, her slender fingers probing for weakness.

"What are you talking about?" He started to laugh along with her. "Just what do you mean I'm not ticklish. At three o'clock in the morning, would anyone be ticklish? Are you?"

With that he pushed Cara over onto her back and started to test her body for weak spots.

"No, Quinn! . . . No. Oh, please don't, I didn't mean it . . . Please!" Her laughter immobilized her, leaving her open to his attack.

"This is fun. Would you call this testing your erogenous zones?" The deep masculine laugh rang out in concert with her pleas to stop. "Which tickles more? This or this?" Experimental touches with his fingers accompanied his questions, causing Cara to laugh uncontrollably. Abruptly both laughter and words stopped as two pairs of lips met in a long kiss, sharing touch and taste in an evocation of sensuous pleasure.

"Oh-h, no more, please. I can't take anymore." Cara put a hand on Quinn's chest to hold him off. "Just put your arms around me and hold me, Quinn. Don't do anything else except hold me."

The man looked at the beautiful woman beside him, not understanding the reason for her request but willing to grant it. He closed his arms around her, resting his chin against her hair, taking in the faint fragrance of roses that scented it. For a moment a frown wrinkled his forehead as he tried to analyze his feelings about this woman. He had been caught in her web since Halloween. The shock of hearing her use another man's name when he had brought her to climax that night had resulted in his deliberate campaign to ensnare her in a similar web. He had thought that seducing her would cure him, allow him to walk away from her. He had had many liaisons before, but none with a woman like Cara, who excited his mind as well as his body. The experience with her was like tasting a delicious hors d'oeuvre before a huge dinner. He had only nibbled the introduction to the meal and had a long way to go before he would sample the dessert.

While Quinn pondered his attachment to the woman beside him, she was examining her feelings about him. She was still trying to understand the ease with which she had allowed him to take control of her body; the pleasure he had given her was beyond anything she had known in her marriage. But that she should have fallen into his arms with so little fight . . .

She had known that this man would have an immeasurable effect on her life. This had been apparent from their first meeting, but she hadn't known how deeply she would respond to him. He was rapidly becoming the center of her universe: she enjoyed his mind, his wit, his strength, his love of life. In fact, now that she was being honest with herself, she could admit to herself that she loved him. It wasn't only the touch of his hands and body that she wanted, but the companionship of his whole being. These past weeks of working with him had shown her the total man and exposed her to his fascinating ways.

"Oh Quinn, I've fallen in love with you," she whispered. "What am I going to do about it?"

The arm that held her didn't move, the eyelids that lay shut didn't quiver, the chest under her hand didn't stop its even rise and fall. The man was asleep.

Cara placed a kiss on the warm skin lying beneath her head, closed her eyes and joined Quinn in slumber.

8

~~~~~~~~~~~~~~~~~~~~~~~~

The sound of movement and the chink of silver against china woke Cara the following morning. She stretched in a long languorous movement, feeling wonderfully satisfied, a smile of repletion curling the corners of her mouth. She reached out, searching for her bedmate, only to hear his voice coming from the other side of the room.

"Open your eyes, sleepyhead. It's after twelve and a bright, sunny day and we've lots of things to do." Warm lips touched hers in greeting, then moved to touch the tip of each breast. "Time to get up, shameless wench . . . no fooling around now." His actions denied his words as he sat down on the bed and put his arms around the soft curve of her waist, bringing her up into a sitting position. "You're gorgeous to watch waking up. Your mouth is like a rosebud opening in the sun." His lips nibbled at hers, then pressed against her mouth in a quick hard kiss. He jumped up, pulling at her hand and forcing her to move from the cocoon of blankets, which fell away from her firm body exposing her nakedness to his laughing eyes.

"If I touch you again, we'll never leave this room today . . . and what will Mrs. Stevens think?" He moved away from the bedside to the table where he had placed a tray with mugs of coffee, sugar and cream. "Your robe is next to you. Now come on over here and have some coffee. Then I'll leave you to shower and dress while I go down to help get breakfast on the table."

"How long have you been up?" Cara loved sharing herself with this man. She took note of his vibrant good looks this morning, his exultant air. "What are you looking so . . . so . . . triumphant about?"

"Why shouldn't I? I had a good night. In fact it was a glorious night, shared with the most exciting creature I've ever met. Shouldn't I feel great?"

He watched a deep crimson blush spread over the translucent skin of her face and chest. "Quinn, don't talk like that. You make me feel like a prize that you've won." Quickly she stood, wrapping the white challis robe around her. "What happened was good, but I don't want you to think it's something that's habitual with me. I don't sleep around." She turned her back to him, not able to watch the derision she was afraid to find on his face.

"Cara, I know you don't. I'm grateful for our night together. I'm not judging you, I'm merely accepting whatever you want to give me." He had moved to her side and turned her toward him, holding her loosely in the circle of his arms. "I can't say I'm not glad it happened or that I don't want to spend more hours in bed with you. But I won't ask for more than you're ready to give." Tenderly he kissed her forehead, then the tip of her nose and finally her lips, without passion. The kiss was like the signing of a pact, his seal on an agreement between the two of them.

Cara trembled with the love she felt for him, knowing that he had the power to give her heaven or hell and there was nothing she could do to help him make the choice. His was the controlling hand.

She leaned against him, uttering a prayer that when this week was over, she would have the strength to leave him. If she didn't, if she stayed, she could easily become enslaved by her love for him.

"Here." Quinn reached for a mug of coffee and handed it to her. "Drink up. I'll meet you downstairs. Wear something woolly and warm. We're going for a walk after we eat. No work until tomorrow."

He waited until she sipped from the mug, then with a pleased smile, he left the room, whistling as he went.

Cara walked to the window, pushing aside the organdy curtains to look out at glittering snow-covered hills and sparkling waters of the lake. The scene was framed by a tall pine tree that stood to one side of the window, some of its branches still laden with last week's snowfall.

She sipped her coffee, enjoying the fragrance and wondering how she was to get through the rest of the week. She hoped that the Laketons would soon make their appearance. As long as she and Quinn were alone together, she would be unable to control the passion that filled her every time they came into contact. His slightest touch took her to the edge of a precipice and only he could bring her safely back. Ever since he'd first made love to her, she had known that this would be the danger; when she signed the contract with his company she had sensed she would fall in love with him.

As she pondered, she pinned her long hair to the top of her head and then slipped out of her robe. She walked into the blue-tiled bathroom, reaching into the shower stall to turn on the water. Could she possibly go against her instincts and become his mistress, his pillow friend? He might want to set her up in an apartment. Could she accept that? The warm water flowed across her face and shoulders. No, never. If she continued to sleep with him it would be on her terms, not his. He could be her lover, for now, but there would be no question of money involved.

She would think about it all later . . . no more agonizing for today. She would enjoy each moment for what it was, and let tomorrow take care of itself.

She stepped out of the shower, reaching for the big bathsheet that hung on the back of the bathroom door. She draped herself in it, using one corner to wipe the moisture from her face, smiling at the memory of Quinn licking away her tears of joy after their first lovemaking the previous night. The banked fires in her body flared momentarily, then simmered down as she put aside thoughts of the night's events.

By the time Quinn's voice floated up from the bottom of the steps, Cara had dressed in tobacco brown wool slacks and a paler brown cowl-necked sweater. She was just putting the finishing touch of coral lipstick on her mouth as she answered him.

"I'm coming, I'm coming. Stop yelling!"

"Yelling! I never yell . . . I call, yodel, vocalize, verbalize, scream even, but never yell. That's vulgar!" His black eyes laughed up at her above a broadly smiling mouth.

"You must have cribbed the whole Thesaurus, or do you carry one tucked into your back pocket?" She ran down the steps into his arms.

"I'd like to carry you in my back pocket." He held her close to him. "Then I'd always have you with me . . . to take out and look at whenever I had the need to enjoy your special beauty." He turned with her, keeping one arm around her waist. "Louisa has made us a scrump-tu-ous breakfast. Do you like blueberry and banana pancakes? And there's maple syrup and sausages and juice and English muffins and pots of coffee all served in a bright, sunny breakfast room that looks out on some of the prettiest scenery in New York State. And you'll have the best man in town for company!"

"The only man in town, you mean," she tossed over her shoulder as she walked into the kitchen and greeted the housekeeper.

"Good morning, Mrs. Williams. You look as though you had a good night."

"I did, Mrs. Stevens. The bed was very comfortable." Cara refused to meet Quinn's eyes, cursing her clear skin, which revealed every flush of color. "I'm so hungry, I could eat a refrigerator full of food." She couldn't bear to look at Quinn, sure that his laughing eyes would set her off. Once more the bubble of joy filled her throat and for a moment the love she felt for him shone from her eyes. Quickly she sat down, lowering her head so as not to betray the true state of her feelings.

"Here now, get yourself some of this food so you'll have plenty of energy for all the walking we're going to do today." A broad grin creased his cheeks as he added, "And all the other things I have planned for us."

"I thought we were supposed to work." Cara looked at Mrs. Stevens who smiled approvingly at the huge portion that Quinn had placed on his plate. "I don't think you're going to be any help, Mrs. Stevens, the way you're looking at this man tells me you'll back him with your last dollar if he asks you to."

"Now, now, you young people just go on and enjoy the fresh air. I don't suppose you get too much of it in that big city you come from."

"Young people! You make yourself sound ancient."

"We-l-l, I'm not ancient, but I'm a lot older than you, Mrs. Williams, and that makes you young."

Such logic was irrefutable, so Cara attended to the stack of pancakes on her plate.

"I'll get on with dinner for tonight. You have a good time, hear?"

The housekeeper left the room, taking with her the slight feeling of constraint that had been bothering Cara. She was self-conscious about her relationship with Quinn and felt that it was necessary to avoid acknowledging it to outsiders. For the moment, she was half afraid to acknowledge it to herself. There was a fragility to the exquisite joy; it could so easily be shattered by the wrong word, the wrong look. The inhibitions of her background and training made it difficult for her to be open about this new facet of her association with Quinn.

She was living a moment out of time, out of the real world. Once the real world intruded, she wasn't sure that she would be able to continue with him in this sexual partnership. At least, she would have this precious week. The final decision could wait a while.

"You're thinking too much, love—just relax and enjoy. There's time enough to think." Quinn covered her hand with his. "Finish your coffee and let's get going. I want to show you my private ice skating pond."

"I'm finished, let's go." Cara jumped up from the table and swirled through the door. She grabbed her parka from the closet and slipped into it before Quinn had a chance to help her.

"Hurry up . . . hurry up," she called to him. "Now you're the slowpoke." She opened the front door and ran out. "Last one down the hill is a marshmallow." She waited until Quinn appeared in the doorway, still fastening the buttons of his shearling jacket. "See you at the bottom of the hill."

With a trill of laughter, the lithe figure took off around the path to the back of the house and then down the hill toward the lake. Before she had reached the halfway mark, he had caught her and tackled her into a deep snowbank.

"You can't get away from me, lady, your legs aren't long enough." He turned her over, looking into her snow-covered, rosy cheeked face. "Now you have good healthy color. No one would ever know that you spend all your time gallivanting around nightclubs and discos."

"Oh-h-h that's unfair. I don't spend my time like that at all. I work very hard . . . my boss is a real Simon Legree. He'd never give me the time to go dancing."

She squirmed out from under his body and dashed to the other side of the pathway, scooping up a handful of snow as she went. "Take that, you chauvinist." The snowball hit his chest.

"A fight, Hmm? Well, if that's what you want, that's what you'll get, woman." Faster than she had imagined possible, Quinn scooped up some snow and formed snowballs in his big, gloved hands, throwing them as quickly as he made them.

"No . . . no . . . not fair. You're bigger than I am," she screamed as she collapsed with laughter. "Truce, I cry truce."

"No way . . . you started the battle, now you have to pay the forfeit."

"Oh you're cruel. If I hadn't slipped I would have beaten you." Wide green eyes looked up at the towering figure from between lashes fringed with snow flakes. "What kind of forfeit? We didn't say anything about a forfeit."

"I'll let you suffer a while wondering about that. You'll find out when we get back to the house. Meanwhile let's go for that walk, witch." He put a hand under one of her arms and hoisted her to her feet. "This way," he said without letting go of her.

"Could you move your hand, please? You're making me walk lopsided holding me like that."

"Ooops, sorry." He moved his hand from beneath

her arm, placing it around her waist. "There, is that better?" he asked, comforting her with a quick kiss on her cheek.

Not wanting to accede, but decidedly more comfortable enfolded in the warmth of Quinn's arm, Cara nodded with a murmured "Mmm."

The path led down to a footbridge that crossed the three lane highway that wound round the lake. On the other side of the bridge was a snow-covered beach bare of footprints.

"Angels—let's make angels," she cried as she ran down to the beach.

"Angels? What's that?"

"Oh, Quinn, didn't you ever make angels when you were a kid?" Excited green eyes turned to him.

"I don't even know what you're talking about," he answered. "Explain."

"It's very easy. First you lie down on the snow." She demonstrated by placing her body carefully on the ground with her head toward the rise of the snowbank. "Then you stretch your arms out to the side like this, with your legs in a straight line," she continued. "And then you make the wings like this." She moved her arms up and down in the snow so that they created a wing-shaped indentation. "And when you stand up, there's the angel . . . Oh I forgot, you have to move your legs from side to side, too." Lightly she rose to her feet and stepped away from the marks she had made in the snow.

"I'll be darned," Quinn said. "It *does* look like the silhouette of an angel. *This* I've got to try."

"Be careful, or you'll spoil the outline," cautioned Cara.

"I feel like a fool." Gingerly Quinn folded his long legs as he squatted, then sat in the snow. As Cara hovered over him, he extended his long limbs and lay back, duplicating Cara's movements. Her giggles brought a mock scowl to his face and suddenly he reached for her leg, pulling it out from under her and toppling her over into his waiting arms. "Now, we can make two angels . . . or better yet, a pair of kissing angels." Without waiting for her reply he placed a commanding hand on the back of her head, forcing her down so that his lips could meet hers.

The measure of force was slight; his victim all too willing to take her punishment, even anxious to help him achieve his goal. Quinn's thrusting tongue met the firm caress of Cara's as his lips moved against hers. The heat they generated warmed them and hastened their fingers to the buttons and zippers of their outer clothing.

"My God, I can't keep my hands off you." He moaned as he reached inside her coat, moving his hands over her back and around to the sides of her body. He found her mouth again as his quick fingers felt the warm firm mounds of her breasts, stroking and thumbing the nipples through the wool of her sweater until they hardened in response.

Cara's hands buried themselves in the hair of his chest, rubbing the thick mat with her fingertips. She let the palms of her hands caress the hard, flat plane of his abdomen, uttering wordless sounds as she responded to his kisses and touch.

Finally, coming up for air, she pulled away from him, breathing rapidly. "This is crazy! We came out here for a different kind of exercise. Let go."

"You're right." Quinn tried to control his breath. "But you're the one who wanted to make angels. If it hadn't been for you, we wouldn't have been flat on our backs in the first place. There's just so much temptation I can resist." His grin twisted her heart.

"Oh you! You're just a troublemaker." After struggling to her feet, Cara rezipped her jacket, her cheeks red from the cold and a sudden shyness.

"I still want to show you my skating pond and then, if you'd like, we can build a snowman."

Cara ran, blood pulsing within her, but her eyes darkened despite her freely ringing laughter. Her joy was more sharply felt because of the anticipated pain of the withdrawal that would follow this interlude. He was like a drug in her system, affecting the way she saw the world, sharpening colors, deepening responses. She knew everything would become flat and uninteresting once he was only a memory; life would be a gray and colorless experience.

She ran with her love. She would relish this moment and let tomorrow do its worst. . . .

Determined to make the most of this enchanted time, Cara spent every minute of the next two days with Quinn. They skated on the rough ice of the pond Quinn had spoken of, skied on the cross-country trails around the area, shared memories in front of the fireplace in the study, and held each other in endless passion through the nights. Despite the fact that Quinn could not seem to get enough of her, never did he utter the word love in his ecstatic murmurings as he brought her to that mindless, consuming ecstasy, the continuing culmination of their lovemaking. And because she was afraid to express the depth of her emotions, Cara, too, left it out of her nighttime whispers.

On the third day after their snowball fight, Mrs. Stevens greeted them with news that the Laketons had contacted her and would be arriving the following day.

"Mrs. Laketon said she hoped you were enjoying your vacation, and that she was anxious to hear some of the ideas for the house."

"And so endeth the respite," Quinn said with a regretful grin. "It's been too short and too good. But now, back to the old grind, right, Cara *mia?*"

"Well, that's what we really came here for. If you want that series to be ready for publication in the fall, we've got to get down to business." She held back until Mrs. Stevens left the room, then crossed over to him, leaning against his body, her arms around his waist. "Amazing how you seduced me without even trying. I fell into your arms like a ripe plum, didn't I?" A laugh masked the shadow of sorrow that had been with her for days. "It's been a lovely time, Quinn . . ." She held her face up, reaching for his lips, then regretfully withdrawing from his embrace. "And so to work; where shall I start?"

"I guess you'd better start getting your notes in order. I know you have lots of ideas you've been jotting down. I think you might do a quick rendering of the master bedroom. That campy, late Victorian look sounded good. Then you might want to do some sketches for the parlor and the dining room. That should give us a satisfactory idea of where we'll be going. I thought I might start visiting some of the antique shops in town to get an idea of what's available. Then if I see anything that I think might interest you we can go back together."

He had moved away from Cara with an effort and forced himself to start thinking in terms of the assignment. "In all honesty, I'm damn sorry that we have to do this. I'd rather kidnap you and take you to an island in the Caribbean where there'd be nothing to do all day except make love."

"Enough!" Cara held a hand up in protest, trying to laugh at him. "It's bad enough that I feel like that, but if my boss feels the same way, how am I supposed to get any work done? You're supposed to give me moral support, so don't be cruel, Quinn." A wry smile twisted her lips. "Now, where did I put my pad?"

Denying her need for his touch with a strength of will that surprised her, Cara continued to talk in a light vein about the work she would accomplish once he left the house. She made some suggestions about the things he should look for on his shopping expedition, then stood at the front door waving as he drove off. She walked back into the study, forcing herself to concentrate on the job, but found her concentration broken almost as soon as she sat on the couch. The soft cushions and shabby fabric seemed to hold the imprint of the passion it had witnessed a short time ago. Cara rested her head against the back of the sofa, revelling in the memory, then shook her head in self-denial. She stood up, grabbed for her pad and pencils and fled the room. The colder atmosphere of the unused dining room would be less distracting to work in.

That night, their lovemaking had overtones of farewell. Quinn seemed to regret the coming arrival of his hosts, but only because their idyll would be interrupted. Cara knew that unless Quinn was prepared to commit himself to love, she would be incapable of continuing the intense exchange they shared. With the greatest of discipline she prevented herself from telling him of the love she felt, but her body, her hands, her wordless mouth made a mute declaration. When at last they fell asleep, near dawn, the tears crept from between her eyelids, mourning the loss she would feel on the morrow.

The Laketons arrived late the next day, and Cara had completed the drawing of the proposed master bedroom and a few quick sketches of concepts for the rooms on the ground floor. She had gone upstairs to shower and change into something more suitable than blue jeans and a sweater when she heard the sound of voices and the clatter of footsteps mounting the uncarpeted stairs.

"Cara, are you dressed?" Quinn's deep voice called to her. "Ted and Judy have arrived." Her door opened before she could answer and the handsome dark-haired man walked in. He stood for a second, taking in her loveliness, then gathered her into his arms to place a deep kiss on her warm and willing mouth. Abruptly, she remembered that they were no longer alone in the house and pushed him away.

"No, don't, Quinn. We can't . . . I wouldn't want your friends to suspect anything. It would . . . I wouldn't feel right." She stood in the center of the room, her flaming red gold hair waving around her face. She was dressed in an ice blue velvet hostess gown with a bateau neck, long sleeves and a wide *obi* sash. The color, cold and sharp, made the pearlescent tint of her skin warmer.

"For the time being," she continued, "we have to act as if there is no more between us than an employer/employee relationship." Her voice was colder than she had intended. She was having trouble with her longing to be in Quinn's arms.

At first he was puzzled. "But Cara, the Laketons are my friends, they wouldn't think any less of you."

"I would think less of me. What happened was a . . . a . . . oh, call it a momentary madness. But I've told you, I'm not comfortable hopping in and out of beds. I made a mistake. It was lovely, but it's over."

The black eyes became frozen, the lean face lost the smile that had warmed its features. "If you had given me a chance, I would have thanked you for your participation in our little distraction, and asked you to forego the pleasures we shared. But thank you for making it so much easier. Now, you needn't suffer the embarrassment of my ending it since you beat me to the punch. If you're quite ready, I'd like to introduce you to my friends." Without waiting for a reply, he left the room, not bothering to see if Cara was following him.

For a moment she stood there in shock, not believing what had just happened. Her shoulders hunched over as she grasped her arms around her middle, trying to protect herself from the pain she felt. He had responded to her change of attitude just as she had feared. But in the long run, it would be easier this way. Dragging out their affair would only wear down the fragile barriers she was building for protection. He had become dearer to her than she could have believed possible, and in so short a time. Yet, looking back, it seemed as though there was never a day when she hadn't known him. The essence of the man seemed to stretch back into her past in an endlessly familiar way, woven in and around her experiences.

It would be difficult to erase that feeling, but, knowing that he involved himself only in short-term romances, she had to erase it. Better that *she* dictate the moment; perhaps it would make it less like major surgery, especially since she was cutting out her heart.

She walked down the stairs toward the sound of voices coming from the large living room. "Oh good, Cara, I've been waiting to introduce you to our hosts, Ted and Judy Laketon. This is Cara Williams, who has fallen in love with your house." The bitter cold of his voice had changed to something more socially accept- able as he made the introductions. "We've started on our drinks, would you like something?"

"Make it a Canadian and gingerale. I feel thirsty tonight," she answered before turning to the newcom- ers to acknowledge the introduction. "I'm so glad you've finally arrived. I've been wanting to tell you how wonderful I think your home is. I hope there was nothing too serious that took you away?"

"Oh no, just some family idiocy. My mother always overreacts and my father screams for help and we're expected to come running to the rescue at a moment's notice." Judy Laketon smiled at Cara as she took her hand in greeting. "We think Quinn's idea of featuring renovations of unusual homes is just terrific . . . especially since we'll be benefiting from your exper- tise. It must be very exciting for you."

"Judy, do you want a refill or shall we take our drinks in to dinner with us?" Ted Laketon broke into the conversation. "Cara, nice to meet you. Quinn's told us that you're one of the most talented designers on his staff. I know it's usually the province of the wife to be involved in the decorating, but this time I'm as interested as Judy." He began to lead the way into the dining room as he spoke. "I guess you're bursting with plans, but I'd like to suggest that we wait until tomorrow to begin. I'm too pooped after all the traveling to take anything in tonight."

Constantly aware of Quinn's presence on her right, Cara managed to join in the dinner conversation, responding to the light chitchat as best she could. Fortunately she felt an immediate rapport with the Laketons, which made everything a little easier. She and Judy discovered a mutual passion for Anne McCaffrey's novels and she found that she shared a lively interest in baseball with Ted. They spent part of dinner comfortably congratulating each other on the New York Yankee's successful season, bemoaning the terrible loss of Reggie Jackson's talents and alternately castigating and hailing George Steinbrenner. Although the conversation flowed easily, at no time did she exchange comments with Quinn.

She felt deprived; the emptiness that remained after their earlier exchange left a void that seemed to loom larger and larger in her future. How long would she be able to keep up this pretense of sociability? How soon could she plead tiredness or a headache to excuse herself from being civil? Would it feel any different to lose a limb? an eye? any physical part of herself?

She had suffered a loss once before, but it had not been as sharply shocking as the loss of Quinn, perhaps because she had had time to get used to the idea of living without Donny. Though she had known Quinn but a short time, their relationship had been intensely, totally satisfying.

"Shall we have liqueurs in the study? The fire should be burning nicely in there by now." Judy's lively eyes were looking at her, waiting for an answer.

"Sorry, I sometimes get involved in an idea and my hearing disappears," Cara replied, excusing her distraction. "I was just thinking about a color scheme for the dining room," she finished weakly.

Her excuse was accepted without further comment, but, because she had been so inattentive, she felt it incumbent upon her to join the Laketons and Quinn for an additional half hour before making her escape.

To her relief, Quinn announced the following morning that he had received an urgent message from his New York office. Rather than drive back to the city, he had made arrangements to fly from the Ithaca airport. He would return by Sunday, in time to drive Cara back to the city.

The next three days passed quickly. Believing she had made the only decision possible, Cara was able to hold back the emptiness left by the misunderstanding between Quinn and herself.

She found a friendship with Judy Laketon that would have been welcome had there been no involvement with Quinn. As it was, she accepted the hospitality that was offered and managed to keep from exposing too much of her sorrow to the older woman.

Judy Laketon, Cara soon learned, was intelligent, good-humored and insatiably interested in the world around her. As their friendship deepened, Cara became more confident that her designs would make the Laketons' home a joyous place to live.

Once they had decided on a tentative color scheme, Cara and Judy spent hours visiting the local auctions and shops, occasionally finding pieces that Judy loved and Cara felt would fit into the new Victorian decor. Finally, Cara felt that she had done as much as possible with her rough plans and could do nothing more until the initial construction was completed. As soon as Quinn returned, they would be on their way to Manhattan where she would place her orders for carpeting, drapes and fabric she had specified.

Sunday arrived and with it the dark-eyed man who had taken possession of Cara's heart. Once more the house seemed to come alive. His deep voice rang through the house as he called out his greetings, sending Cara into a moment of remembrance that quickly brought tears to her eyes.

They met at the lunch table; Cara sure that her anguish was obvious to the people present. She was unaware that her efforts to maintain her equanimity masked her inner torment with an immobility of feature and an uncharacteristic coldness in her green eyes.

"Ted and Judy tell me you've come up with a fine plan for the house. I understand you've been working very hard." Quinn's voice was expressionless; he could have been commenting on the weather.

"They've made it very easy for me, they like

everything I do." A meaningless laugh punctuated her statement.

A rush of words from Judy about the visits to the auction house took the burden of conversation from Quinn and Cara. Cara pushed the food around on her plate and found her appetite had become nonexistent.

"Will you be all packed and ready to leave by eight in the morning?" Quinn addressed the question to Cara. "I'd like to get back to the city by mid afternoon."

"No problem, Quinn. If somebody wakes me at seven I'll be all ready." Cara got up to pour more coffee for herself. "It's going to be fun finishing this job. It's a dream of an assignment. I want to check the color samples with you, Judy, for your approval before we leave." Ignoring Quinn, she returned to the table and continued her conversation with Judy.

Later that evening, Ted and Quinn went out for a walk, leaving Judy and Cara sitting in front of the fireplace in the study.

"I get the strangest feeling that you and Quinn are at war with each other," the hostess commented. "Not that you fight, but it's as though there's a curtain between you and instead of opening it, you're each adding layers to make it thicker. Do you want to talk about it?"

Cara couldn't answer immediately. Her voice would have quivered and the tears that lay so close to the surface would have spilled out. She shook her head, shrugged her shoulders and said, "Thank you for caring, it's a case of a head-on collision. We have very different definitions of happiness and he won't change and I can't change. Not to worry . . . I appreciate your concern, you've become more than an acquaintance, but there's nothing anyone can do."

"I'm sure you don't want any remarks from me, but that man is an idiot. He had an unfortunate marriage more than ten years ago and still holds it against all women . . . except me, and he's not romantically interested in me." Judy's face broke into a comic grin. "What's the old saw? We can't live with 'em and we can't live without 'em."

The conversation lapsed between the two women and as soon as the men returned Cara excused herself, saying her goodbyes.

She lay awake for hours, astonished at how much she missed Quinn. She had spent a sum total of four nights in bed with him, but her attraction was so strong that she felt as though he had been her partner for years. She told herself that time heals all wounds, but she had her doubts. Mentally, she began to compose her letter of resignation; she had already worked for Quinn for almost six weeks, another six weeks would fulfill her obligation to work for three months. She would have to stay away from him as much as possible during the time remaining. But she would be so busy completing this project that that should prove easy.

The next morning, she and Quinn were on the road at the anticipated time. There was silence in the car for the first hour or so, Cara trying to doze so that she wouldn't have to talk. They were just passing Scranton, heading for Route 80, when Quinn pulled off the highway and into the parking lot of a nearby diner.

"Why are we stopping?" Cara sat up to look around.

"Let's get some coffee. I wasn't hungry at breakfast, but I could go for a roll or a doughnut now." Quinn got out of the car to walk around to Cara's side. She watched him move, relishing the long lean look of him. He was dressed in a charcoal gray pin-striped suit with a pale gray shirt and gray tie with a maroon design. He had the look of power and success—a man who knew where he was going. And he's not going with me, whispered Cara's mind.

She waited until he opened her door, having become accustomed to his courteous manner, then stepped out and walked ahead of him into the diner.

They chose a table and sat down. Quinn waved away the menus held out by the waitress, ordering two coffees and two sweet rolls.

"This week has been hell, Cara. You know that, don't you?" His eyes were angry, his face seemed to have new lines of strain.

"I'm sorry, Quinn. I don't know what I can do to make it any easier." Her clear green eyes shimmered behind a veil of tears. "I assure you, this is as difficult for me as it is for you. Although why it should be difficult for you is more than I can understand."

"More than you can understand! What are you talking about? Don't you know what we shared? Didn't you feel the same thing that I did?" His voice was harsh with emotion.

"Of course I know, maybe even more than you do, but I can't live like this! I can't be your lover, pillow friend, mistress . . . whatever you want to call it, and be a business associate at the same time. The cost is too great. And for my own protection, I've decided that at the present time the job is more important than an affair that may be over in a month or two or even six." Quinn's face paled as she spoke, but he made no move to interrupt her as she continued. "I guess I'm out of step with the times, but I'm a one-man woman, and I need the full commitment of the man to whom I give my trust . . . and love." She'd said it without meaning to, she'd told him how she felt.

He sat silently as the waitress served the coffee and rolls, spooning sugar into his cup when she had left.

"I think you're a fool. No, that's too strong a word. I think you're wrong to make that kind of a decision. We could have a wonderful time, Cara. We're good together, not just in bed but in every way. I enjoyed those three days like nothing before and I want many more like them. It's the same at the office—I like to bounce my ideas off you; you're like a sounding board. But I won't beg or plead. You have to be the one to make the decision."

"Didn't you hear me, Quinn? I said I love you. And I would want a family, and a home and the pride a wife can take in her husband, in the sharing of a life together—sharing all the troubles and triumphs, the good times and the bad, making each other stronger, giving each other love. If I can't have all that, Quinn, I'll do without. For me half a loaf isn't better than none." She looked down at her hands clasped together on the table top as though in prayer. "I know what we had together, Quinn, and I won't cheapen it by letting the insecurities of a part-time relationship tarnish it. In the end the pain of a breakup would be worse than what's happening today." She looked at him, her eyes brimming with sorrow. "No, Quinn. Half a loaf won't do. It would only leave me hungry for more."

"O.K. Cara, if that's the way you want to play the game, we are simply business associates. I won't ask you for more than that, but it had better be the best you've got to give."

9

Cara took out her key to unlock the door to the apartment. The trip back from Ithaca seemed to have been endless. Quinn had spoken only a few times after that coffee stop outside Scranton, and then only about matters pertaining to the magazine. He had dropped her at the Greenwich Village address with no further reference to her decision to unequivocally end their short-lived affair.

To her relief, Jenny had not yet returned home and Cara was able to collapse on the couch without going into the explanations she knew her roommate would require.

Looking back on the first few days of the trip, Cara was astonished at her immediate capitulation to Quinn's seduction. She had practically fallen over herself in her eagerness to get into bed with him. Now she'd have to pay the consequences for having fallen in love as well.

He was like an addiction. Denying herself the touch of his hands, the warmth of his body, the passion of his lovemaking, was like denying herself her hearing, her sight, her life. As she sat looking blankly at the wall opposite, Cara knew that she had no choice but to resign as soon as possible. If she handed in her resignation immediately, she would be able to avoid the Virginia trip to the Contessa's home and could devote her remaining time to finishing the Laketon house.

Then she'd be free. Free to lick her wounds for however long it would take to get rid of this longing for—what had Jenny called him?—an eleven on a scale of one to ten.

The sound of a key turning in the lock broke the silence, then Jenny's voice was calling, "Cara, are you here? I didn't expect you until later. How are you?"

"Hi, Jenny, I'm fine, a little tired." Cara managed to summon a smile at the sight of Jenny's pixie face. "How'd the week go for you? Anything exciting happen?"

Jenny began to rattle on about events at the Institute and various dates with Rick. She flitted back and forth about the apartment, putting things away, inspecting the kitchen shelves for food and choosing records for the stereo.

"Oh, I meant to tell you, Robert called. He asked that you get in touch with him as soon as you got back. Something about the wrong fabric being used on some chair or other." Jenny curled up in the arm chair, eating a spoonful of yogurt as she spoke.

"I'll call him in a while. God, I'm exhausted." Cara sank back into the soft pillows. "I'm glad to be home."

"Why are you so tired? I thought you'd come back all rested and lively. Being out of the city is a vacation even when it's work, especially in your job." The blonde head tilted with a questioning air. "How's superman? Did you have fun with him?"

"Oh yeah, great fun." The ready tears appeared in Cara's eyes. She took a deep breath to steady herself. "It was a bit more complicated than I had expected."

Jenny missed the inference in Cara's statement and went on questioning her about her week. "What were the people like? I've always wanted to see that part of the state. One of these days Rick and I are going to go camping up there. The state parks are supposed to be breathtaking."

As Cara listened to her roommate she felt years older than Jenny. If only she could go through life like the bubbly blonde, skimming along the top of experiences without becoming emotionally involved. Even Jenny's relationship with Rick was so casual—they were like a pair of puppies jumping at anything that would offer them "fun." Not that Jenny wasn't a dear, always wanting Cara to participate with equal zest, but she seemed so young, so very young.

"Hey, Jen, would you mind if I did a disappearing act? I'm absolutely exhausted. Quinn wanted to leave early this morning so I was up early. If I don't get some sleep, I'll be a walking zombie tomorrow."

"No, you go ahead. Can I help with your unpacking? I have to finish the dress I'm going to wear in the fashion show, so don't bother about me." Jenny carefully picked up the empty yogurt carton and lid, stuffing the used napkin inside the container. "Do you want to get up for dinner or will you try to sleep through the night?"

"If I wake up in time to eat I'll yell, but if you have plans to go out, don't bother about me. I'll see you in the morning." Cara picked up her bag and moved to her bedroom. She felt as though she had been gone a thousand days. The old familiar furnishings were a comfort to see; their presence reminded her of less complicated times and were soothing to her spirit.

Tiredly she took off her clothes, falling into bed without bothering to wash her face or take down her hair. Once more she was sleeping alone, but this time the loneliness was worse than before. She fell into a welcome sleep, escaping the bitter memories.

Consciousness returned the next morning when Jenny's hand on her shoulder shook her. "Cara, it's after seven, c'mon now. You've slept thirteen hours. It's time to get up."

Reluctantly, green eyes opened to the new day. "Okay, Jen, I'm awake. Gosh, I really conked out, didn't I?" Her voice, still drugged with sleep, was slow.

"If I go make coffee will you get up?"

"Yes, okay . . . swell. You make coffee. I'm up, I'm up." Cara sat up to prove her point. "Good morning. Thanks for waking me. I guess I never set the alarm last night. I didn't think I'd sleep so soundly."

"Obviously you were tired. Hurry up now."

Jenny hurried out of the room, her fuzzy red slippers flapping as she walked. Cara smiled at the sight of the diminutive blonde in her nightshirt and footwear.

She did feel better today. Maybe it would go more

easily than yesterday. Working in the office wouldn't necessarily put her in Quinn's company that much. She'd finish the renderings and start making calls to track down some of the furniture, and . . .

Making plans for her day kept thoughts of Quinn out of her mind. By the time she had donned the trim navy suit with the pale blue georgette blouse and her gray suede boots, and sprayed herself with *Tearose* perfume, she was ready to face the world.

She walked into her office with a gay "Hi!" as she passed her secretary. "Bring me all the news that's fit for early morning consumption in fifteen minutes please, Myra."

"Sure thing, Cara. A Mr. Avery has been trying to get in touch with you. Do you want to return his call right away, or shall I just give you the number?"

"Give me a few minutes then ring him for me, will you?" She might as well get the call to Robert over with. He'd want to see her and in a sense she owed him an evening, but not yet. He'd only start to press her about marriage, and she couldn't face that now. It was ironic—she felt about Quinn the way Robert felt about her, and neither could fulfill their needs. It was really too bad that she couldn't have fallen in love with the professor. They were compatible in so many ways, but not in the important ones.

As she had expected, the conversation with Robert was difficult. Despite her effort to avoid a date with him, she found herself agreeing to meet him for dinner the following evening. She knew that she would excuse herself from further contact at that time. It wasn't fair to keep dragging on a fruitless friendship like this.

Later that day, Cara was dictating some letters to Myra when Quinn walked into her office through the connecting door. For a moment, she thought she would be unable to control her expression, that he would look at her face and immediately know how she felt, but her discipline was greater than she knew.

"Good morning, Quinn," she greeted him softly, then looked pointedly at the mass of papers in his hand. "Do you need my help for something?"

"Yes, I want you to go over this correspondence and tell me what you make of it. It's from that Italian furniture firm that Paolo Monti designs for; we're supposed to be featuring his new work in our June issue." Quinn's concentration was totally on the problems of the magazine. No trace of personal regard was in his voice. "He's going to be here next month and we're entertaining him."

"*We're* entertaining him?"

"Uh-h yes, I have to talk to you about that. Myra, how about getting yourself a cup of coffee?" A charming grin accompanied his suggestion. "Cara and I need some privacy."

"Sure, boss. I'm on my way." A saucy smile from the gray-haired woman answered Quinn's wink as the secretary left the office.

"I wish you wouldn't do that, Quinn. I feel like a fool when you play games like that with Myra. God knows what she'll make of that 'privacy' bit." Cara's tone was cold.

"I didn't think you'd care to have her hear the conversation we're about to have." His tone was icy. "About this Paolo . . . you'll be needed to act as my hostess during his visit. You'll have to plan at least one dinner party in my home and perhaps two at restaurants. He was very hospitable when I was in Italy and I must return that hospitality."

"But why me? He'll misconstrue our relationship if I act as hostess in your home. I won't do it! That's not part of my contract. I signed up to design, not to act as your wife, *pro tem*. It's impossible, impossible."

"I hate to remind you, but you were hired as my assistant. Since I need *assistance* in this matter, it comes within the responsibilities of the job." Black eyes glared at her. "You needn't worry about anything personal prompting my request. I don't force what's not wanted, Mrs. Williams. I need a hostess and you're the logical choice. If you need anything special to wear, charge it to the company. It will be treated as though it were a uniform." He paused, waiting for her response as though he expected an explosion.

To his surprise, Cara controlled her initial reaction and in a quiet, noncommittal voice she agreed to his request, asking what other plans he wished her to make.

"You'd better book at least one show. Try for Wednesday evening, and . . . let's see, he'll be here for seven nights. Two of them will be spent with his relatives in Connecticut, one will be the dinner at home, one the play and dinner, another will be dinner and maybe disco, and try for the ballet for the sixth evening. That will leave one evening for rest and relaxation and then we'll be able to ship him back to Milan." A smile crossed his face at the picture he had conjured up, and Cara was caught in it before she knew what was happening. Once again, that nameless, timeless sharing was there. Their minds understood, their bodies responded and there was a surge of feelings that was almost palpable. Then, just as quickly, each exerted control and the moment passed.

"I'll agree to go along with this as long as there's complete understanding on your part that being a hostess does not include any personal prerogatives like sharing a bed." Privately she admitted she would love to share his bed, his life, everything that was his. But she couldn't let him guess at her feelings. She'd made her choice and she would stick with it. It wouldn't be for much longer now.

"You haven't been asked for that service, Cara, so don't worry about it." The knowing eyes looked at her again, eyebrows raised in a mocking slant. "Unless you're putting in a bid for a place in my bedroom? We could always resume our alliance."

"That was unnecessary, Quinn. If you want my cooperation, don't throw innuendoes around. I won't stand for it." She rose from her chair and began to walk about the office. "I'll make all the arrangements, but I want it understood that since you insist on this association, you will at least treat me politely."

"I agree to your terms." Clearly he was bored with the whole thing. "And now, if you'll excuse me . . . let me know when you want to see the apartment. You'd better arrange for a caterer."

Without a further exchange of words, Quinn left Cara's office. She was left feeling angry, frustrated and fearful. She suspected some trick in this ploy of Quinn's. His manner had been cold, but there had been a hint of something there, something other than the anger he had displayed when she'd first refused to continue their intimate relationship.

She stood, leaning against her desk, thinking about her options. What could he do to tie her to his side? Finally she pressed the buzzer and called her secretary back into the office. She would hand in her resignation right away. Then she'd work like a fiend to finish the Laketon plans. If she really concentrated, she was sure she could get the advance work done in less than two weeks. It would take eight to ten weeks for orders to be filled, but by then she would be able to freelance whatever time would be needed in Ithaca to complete the project. It would not be necessary to be in this office for those weeks; she could be far from here with no chance of meeting Quinn.

She moved back to her chair, saying to Myra as she walked into the room, "I have a very important letter for you, Myra. I'll need three copies."

The last curtain call had been taken and the house lights had come up as the audience gradually moved out of the jewel-like State Theater at Lincoln Center. Paolo Monti was leaving for Italy the following day and he, Quinn and Cara had attended a performance of the American Ballet Theatre that evening. The preceding five days had been a whirlwind of activity for Cara, alternating between her crowded daytime work and the glittering social evenings. Thank goodness this was the end of Paolo's visit and tomorrow would be her last day at *Domestic Design*.

When Quinn had received her letter advising him of her determination to leave the magazine, he had raged, but she was adamant in her decision, unable to bear the pain of the half life she had as his assistant. She had indicated that she would be available for the final installation of furnishings at the Laketons, and would make arrangements directly with Judy. Her desk was almost all cleared out and the lovely green living room/office would be empty of her presence by five p.m. the following afternoon.

"Shall we stop for a drink . . . Cara, Quinn? I would like to, this one last time. You have made my visit here so pleasant, I should like to toast you with a fine wine tonight." The short, excitable designer took each of them by an elbow, hugging them in his exuberance. "Oh, I love this city . . . almost as much as I love Milano. Where else does one find such excitement, such beauty, such . . . goings-on?"

"Paolo, you should have been a gossip columnist. I think you've spent a good part of your time here reading those rags that dignify themselves with the name 'newspaper.' You know there's very little truth in what you read in them."

"Oh yes, my dear Quinn, but it is such spicy untruth. I admit, it is . . . what you call it . . . yellow journalism, *sì?* But I love it . . . that is my weakness. I love it even more when someone sues for slander and wins. Then I feel righteous indignation on the part of that person. That is the best time, *non è vero?*"

Cara laughed as she pulled her arm from the grip of the Italian. "I'd love to have a drink with you, but I have an early call to make tomorrow, Paolo. I'm going to get a cab and take myself home. It's been such fun this week . . ." She started to say her goodbyes.

"We'll drop you off, no need to take a cab." Quinn grasped her arm to lead her to the long gray limousine with the uniformed chauffeur. "Paolo, I don't think you realize that you'll have to be up very early to get everything done before you leave.

"Maybe we'd better postpone that drink until you can offer it to us in Milan." He swept his companions into the car without waiting for their comments.

"Really, Quinn, this is unnecessary. I could just as easily have flagged a cab," Cara protested.

"At this hour, with all the theatres letting out? There isn't an empty cab in sight and I won't leave you alone on the street," Quinn answered, then turned away to speak to Paolo.

Cara sat mutely, remembering the first time she had been in this car. If it hadn't been for that stupid taxi accident and the spiked punch, she would never have found herself so torn apart. But then, she would never have experienced such love either. Less than twenty-four hours and then she could go away, start afresh where she would not be reminded of Quinn.

The car drew to a stop and Paolo began to clamber out. Cara awoke to the realization that Quinn had instructed his driver to stop at the hotel first; leave it to him to create an awkward situation. Now she'd have to face saying goodnight to him alone.

"I want to make a stop at the office for a moment," he said as the car began once more to move through the traffic. "I won't be in tomorrow, so you'd better come up and show me what you've done about arranging for deliveries and so forth. I'll have to instruct someone . . ."

She listened to his voice, examining it for hidden meanings. Then she laughed at herself. What could he do? He wasn't a monster, the most he might try would be a farewell kiss, and from the sound of his voice she doubted whether even that was on the agenda.

"All right, I might as well. I'll have enough to do tomorrow," she said agreeably. "Have you begun interviewing for another assistant?"

"No, I've put it off for a while. I may just assign each project to someone already on staff. That way we'll get a variety of tastes for input." He leaned back against the seat and shut his eyes, closing her out, as though he couldn't bear to look at her. "God, it's been a hectic week. That man is incredible. He even squeezed in a trip to the Statue of Liberty and the Empire State Building. He felt he owed it to his children to be able to tell them about it, and he's not married, nor has he any offspring! Incredible."

"Why is it incredible? Because he feels an obligation to the family he *might* have? Obviously he thinks in terms of family . . . something you don't seem capable of doing." Cara looked away from the glowering face. "Why am I having this discussion with you? I knew I should have insisted on taking a cab. You are impossible."

The car had stopped for a traffic light. Cara reached for the door handle, intending to get out before the light.

"Oh no, you don't." Quinn's arm reached out and his strong hand gripped her wrist before she could put any pressure on the handle. "I'll see that you get home. And I'll stop the talking. Just don't try to get out of the car, Cara." He pulled her back onto the seat, moving away from her so that there was space between them. "It's been a nice evening up 'til now . . . don't spoil it."

There was no further discussion until they reached the building that housed the magazine offices. Politely, Quinn asked her once more to accompany him to the tower floor so she could give him the necessary information.

"If I have to I will," she responded grudgingly. "But I don't know why it couldn't have waited until tomorrow."

"I told you, I won't be in tomorrow. This won't take long, I promise." As they walked into the building, he smiled beguilingly and her wall of armor began to melt.

Frightened by her immediate capitulation to his charm, she moved away from him in the closeness of the elevator. The brush of her taffeta skirt against his trousers as she walked out of the elevator caused a tremor that shot through her body.

Quickly she walked down the corridor to her office, flipping light switches as she went. His voice called out, telling her that he had to stop in his office for a moment before joining her to go over the papers.

The stillness that pervaded the building enfolded her in a timeless atmosphere. When Quinn came through the door, his jacket off and his tie hanging loose around his neck, there was a sense of inevitability to the moment. As his agile fingers undid the buttons of his shirt, she could feel her breath slow and her heart beat more rapidly.

She stood clutching her silver envelope bag to her chest, as though it might protect her. Her eyes had become huge in the pallor of her face, pallor that rivaled the white chiffon halter she was wearing.

I must do something, say something. "The folder

is over here in the cabinet. Just let me get the key to . . . to . . ."

"What's the matter, too many memories for you, Cara love?" How could a voice that had once been so caressing be so cold?

"No." His lack of warmth helped her regain her composure. "No, I keep the memories locked away, Quinn. They're too precious to take out just any old time. Now, shall we get to work?" She was able to speak briskly, having once more sealed herself away from him.

"That's what we're here for. Bring out the plans." He switched on the desk lamp and waited until she had opened the cabinet and taken out the needed folders.

"Do you have any fruit juice in the refrigerator?" he asked.

"What for?"

"I'd like a drink . . . don't be inhospitable."

Impatiently Cara found him some orange juice, making disapproving noises when he asked for some vodka as well.

"I didn't come up here for a party, Quinn. It won't make the work any easier if you have a drink."

"Don't worry." Once more he was laughing at her. "The vitamins in the juice counteract the alcohol; ergo, no effect."

"As I said before, you're impossible. How do you expect me to do any work with you in such a mood?"

"You're the one in the mood. Are you in the mood, Cara? Would you like me to do this?" He had moved close to her as he spoke and leaned toward her, touching her lips with his when he finished his question. "Or this?" His mouth moved to her neck. "Or this?" It made contact with her ear.

Her knees turned to water at the first touch of his lips. In spite of her resolution not to succumb, her body refused to accept the orders of her mind. "Oh no . . . please don't . . ." she sighed as she went limp with emotion.

His arms caught her before her knees buckled, bringing her tightly against his body. Again his lips captured hers, this time ravishing them, punishing them. As he held her with one arm, his other hand began to caress her shoulder, bared to its touch by the cut of her blouse. The questing fingers moved to her neck and then down to the decolletage of her top. One long finger insinuated itself under the fabric, reaching for the already hardened nipples, caressing them in a way that lit a fire in her blood.

Helplessly, her arms closed around him, her hands pulling at his shirt, seeking the warmth of his skin. She writhed against him, wanting only to get closer as the thrust of his tongue filled her mouth, playing a miniature version of the game their bodies would play. She moaned against the harshness of his mouth, mindless, aware of nothing but the flames burning inside her.

He lifted her into his arms, tightening his grip as he carried her to the white velvet couch. He stood her on her feet, unzipping her skirt, removing her blouse, as he said, "Take my clothes off, Cara. Undress me. I want to kiss you and touch you and make love to you. God, I need you, Cara, just like you need me."

He had loosened his hold on her to free his hands.

The import of his words broke the spell that held her and she suddenly pushed herself away from him with a violent shove.

"No! You indescribable son of a . . ." Her eyes blazed with passion; not the passion of sexual need, but the passion of anger and self-hate. "I trusted you, and look what you're doing."

"You can't tell me you don't want me as much as I want you."

"Want . . . need . . . is that *all* you ever think of? Don't you ever think of love and truth between two people?" Cara began to laugh quietly. "I once told you I loved you . . . and it didn't mean anything, did it? You set up this whole thing—the evenings with Paolo, this trip here tonight, just to get your way. I could even call it an exercise for your pleasure." She threw his shirt at him. "Here put this on, you might catch cold. I want to tell you something I found out tonight, Quinn, thanks to you. I found out that you are no longer an eligible man from my point of view.

"You are a dishonest lover. You may take the time to give as much pleasure as you receive, but you don't really care for your partner. You couldn't accept that I don't wish to continue the relationship on your terms, so you chose to trick me into continuing without giving me the option to accept or refuse. You're despicable. I can hardly believe that the man I thought I loved is such a paper hero."

Almost in tears by now, Cara continued to keep a tight rein on herself as she straightened her clothes and tidied her hair.

"I reached out to you, thinking to find the man you seemed to be; someone tender, loving, warm. But you're not like that. You're afraid and cold, too frightened by the ghost of your past to reach out to a better future. Well, you can live your life without commitment if you want. I can't. The funniest part of this whole mess is that I wasn't even looking for a wedding ring from you. I missed you so much I would have accepted whatever kind of a twosome you wanted us to be, if you had only told me you loved me. And you couldn't even make that kind of commitment. You really are an empty person, Quinn, and I feel sorry for you."

Cara grabbed her purse and ran from the room.

Quinn, confronted suddenly by a picture of himself that he had never seen, was unable to move. He heard the elevator doors close; the sound released him from the frozen stance and he sank down onto the couch. For the first time in his life he felt totally alone. Something precious had gone out of his life.

10

Cara finished patting the soil around the roots of the iris clump she had just planted. The late May sun was warm on her back and her exertions had brought beads of perspiration around her hairline. She wiped at her forehead with a grubby hand, leaving a streak of the rich soil on her white skin.

"Oh, it's so good to feel the sun like this. I think I'll take my paints down to the harbor later and work on my painting." She spoke to her aunt who had been clipping away at the lilac bush with her pruning shears. "I can't believe I've been able to complete enough canvases to have a showing. It was awfully nice of Helen to do this for me."

"Of course it was nice, but she wouldn't have offered you a show if she hadn't thought she'd be able to sell the paintings. She's not in the gallery business for love, my dearie . . . profit, and lots of it, is the driving force behind her." Norma put down the shears and removed the gardening gloves. "I think we've been working out here long enough. How about some lunch?"

"What's on the menu? I hope it's something filling, I'm really hungry today. It must be the crisp New England air." Cara stood up and began to walk with Norma toward the side door of the house. "Do I have time for a shower, do you think, or is the food all ready to be served? I never know with you . . . you're such a magician in the kitchen. I sometimes think that you can prepare a meal just by sending your thoughts to the kitchen."

"Not quite . . . but thanks for the kind words." The older woman opened the door and preceded Cara into the house. "You run along and shower, I'll get the food on the table. As long as you don't take too long, both you and lunch should reach the table at the same time."

"Ummm, you're the greatest, Norma. I'll be right down." She placed a quick kiss on the soft skin of her aunt's face and then ran up the stairs to the dormered room that had been hers for the past five weeks.

The calm, cherishing love that her aunt had shown her had done much to ease Cara's pain after she had left New York and Quinn. She now could think of him without breaking down in tears as she had for the first ten days. She knew that she would never wholly recover from the impact he had had on her life, but she also believed that the day would come when she would be able to turn to someone else for the love she hoped to have again.

At present, her aunt was allowing her to enjoy the

peaceful period of the presummer quiet in this lovely coastal resort. She had spent many hours at the beach, painting or sketching the sharply angled rock formations and lobster boats. She had made still life compositions from lobster pots, marker buoys and net that had given her further scope for her talents. She had been able to hold back the pain by concentrating on her art, and perhaps that pain had even helped her develop a richer, more mature palette and interpretation.

She had told Norma about the affair with Quinn, had gone over and over their attraction for each other. She had tried, with Norma's help, to understand more completely the man's incapacity to commit himself to more than a surface relationship. Eventually she had concluded that there was a flaw in his makeup that would never be overcome, and was then able to be thankful she had escaped further hurt by ending their connection.

Freshly showered and dressed in her favorite corduroy pants and matching teal blue sweatshirt, Cara sat down to the delicious chowder her aunt had prepared for lunch. "Uh-oh, there goes my waistline," she said as she spooned up the creamy soup with its floating bits of chopped clams and potatoes. "This is New England chowder at its best. When I leave here, I'm taking some of your recipes with me. I just have to pin you down so you can start dictating."

"It's the easiest thing in the world to make. When you pin me down I'll tell you the secret!" Norma smiled at her niece. Cara looked a good deal better today then she had when she'd first arrived. Whether she'd look equally well by the end of the day was questionable. It was Norma's dearest wish that she would look even better, but that would have to wait for their visitor's arrival. Norma hoped that Cara would have reason to thank her once she had spoken with him. He had been so apologetic and so earnest when he spoke over the telephone yesterday. Normally she wouldn't interfere, but if she didn't, who would?

"Norma, Norma, where are you?" Cara's voice broke into Norma's reverie. "What on earth were you thinking about? Your forehead was all wrinkled and you looked . . . I don't know . . . Is anything the matter?"

"Oh, love, I forgot to tell you. I spoke to Mrs. Kalens on the phone while you were in the shower. She's the owner of that craft gallery up in Bar Harbour and she told me she'd have to have a delivery of pottery right away. There was an accident and she's lost most of my pieces." Norma looked at Cara to see how she was reacting to the news. "I told her I'd pack up the car and drive up there right away. It's quite a trip, so I may have to stay overnight. Will you mind?"

"But, I'll come with you. It'll be fun to drive up there; I haven't been to Bar Harbour in years."

"Oh no . . . you can't." The words jumped from Norma's mouth. "I mean . . . I'd love to have you come, but I have to ask you to stay here. I'm expecting a delivery of clay and chemicals either this afternoon or tomorrow morning and since it's coming from . . . Boston, I can't ask them to delay it until I get back." Norma looked eagerly at her niece for signs of agreement. "You do understand, don't you?"

"Of course." Not a hint of doubt showed in Cara's face. She accepted her aunt's story unconditionally.

Happy for this unexpected sale, she sent Norma off to pack her wares while she tidied the kitchen.

The cartons of pottery were packed in Norma's van and instructions given about any emergencies that should arise. A hug and a kiss were exchanged and Norma drove off to Bar Harbour. The afternoon was too far gone for Cara to pursue her plans to go painting, so she decided to be lazy and lie in the sun until the late afternoon chill sent her indoors.

The peace of the garden was heavenly, she decided, with the humming of the bees and the sound of the birds. Off in the distance she could hear a lawnmower being used, probably for the first time this season. Daffodils and tulips bordered the white picket fence that surrounded the property, their bright yellow and reds like pennants in the gentle spring breeze.

Heavy eyelids sank down over soft green eyes as sleep overcame Cara. Her breathing slowed and her head sank sideways to rest against her arm. She did not hear the car door slamming and footsteps on the gravel walk that led to the garden. She was unaware of the tall, dark-haired man who stood gazing at her with a warmth in his black eyes.

Quinn pulled over a webbed chair so that he could sit and watch Cara sleep. He was impatient for her to waken but not yet ready to attempt his wooing. Finally he could no longer resist and took her hand in his.

"Cara . . . Cara," he called her name softly. "Open your eyes, Cara." His fingers stroked her hand, pushing the knit cuff of her shirt up her arm so that he could move his hand to clasp her wrist.

"Um-m-m . . . What is it . . . who . . ." Slowly she raised her long lashes and a flash of joy sparkled in the lambent depths of her eyes. Just as quickly as it had flashed, it dulled and a coldness replaced it. "Quinn, what are you doing *here?*" She pulled her hand away from him, shocked that his magic still controlled her. If she allowed him to touch her again, she'd be lost . . . in spite of all her resolves.

"I came by invitation."

"I don't understand. Whose invitation?"

"Your Aunt Norma's of course. Who else is there who would extend an invitation for me to come here?" Little laugh lines creased the corners of his bold black eyes.

"No! Why would she invite you?" Cara refused to look at the face she so loved.

"Maybe because I asked her to."

"I told you I didn't want to see you, Quinn. Go away." Cara lifted herself from the lounger, swinging her legs to the side away from Quinn and putting the chair between them as though it could protect her. "I don't want to talk to you. Go away." She began to walk toward the house.

"This is a lovely garden," he remarked, changing the subject. "Have you been digging in it? Did I ever tell you about the garden at my home in Putnam County? You'd like it."

How could Norma do this to her . . . and without any warning? She was furious at the older woman's ploy, furious at Quinn's unexpected arrival and more than furious at herself to find that she still responded to him like a *mindless idiot.* She wouldn't talk to him . . . then he'd leave. But what if he didn't? What if he followed her into the house? He was so much bigger than she, she'd never be able to get him out without help. And who could she call on for help? The only one she'd trusted had betrayed her.

"You can't come into the house, so go away. I didn't ask you here and I don't want to have anything to do with you, so please, please leave. You've caused me enough grief, I don't want anymore." Her clear green eyes blurred with tears.

"I won't try to come in. I don't want to make you unhappy." The vibrant voice was low. "But I must talk with you. There are so many things I have to say. Please hear me out." He paused for a moment waiting for her to speak. When she offered no answer, he continued: "Have dinner with me tonight. We'll eat at the noisiest, most crowded restaurant you want. Just say you'll join me."

Reluctantly, after studying his face, Cara agreed. "As long as you promise that you won't try anything afterwards. If I had a car I wouldn't even let you call for me, but I haven't. I'll take a taxi home."

"If that's what you want to do, it's fine by me, as long as we spend some time together." He held the door open for her. "I'll be back in about two hours. Will you call for a reservation or shall I? I'm not familiar with the area, where shall we go?"

"I'll call The Captain's. That's the only place that'll be open on a week night at this time of the year." She pulled the door away from him as she stepped through. "I'll be ready." She closed the inner door without waiting for his response, no longer able to keep her composure.

She watched him through the curtained side window as he stood, looking at the closed door. She watched until he finally turned and walked away, an indefinable difference in his attitude. Her brow creased in puzzlement as she tried to understand what that difference was. For one thing his posture . . . he didn't have that jaunty, conquering attitude. For another— she peered at him again through the curtain—he looked defeated.

Was it possible that Quinn had changed . . . that he had missed her enough to begin to . . . No, impossible. Unthinkable. He'd never give up his lifestyle for her. Probably it had something to do with the magazine. Maybe business wasn't going well. It would be too bad if there were problems like that for him, but he had the will to carry him through anything, so why should she worry about him? He certainly hadn't worried about her.

Suddenly she felt a lightening of her spirits; she whirled away from the door, lifting her arms in a free, joyous gesture. What should she wear tonight? She had two hours to make herself absolutely ravishing. Cara, you're back to that insanity again. Don't be too optimistic or you'll fall flat on your face! Paying no attention to the voice of common sense, Cara went to her room to rummage through her wardrobe, hoping to find a dress that would lend her the magical qualities she was sure she would need this evening.

She took a long bubble bath while her hair was rolled in hot curlers. Once out of the tub, she sprayed herself with her favorite *Tearose* eau de cologne, then carefully applied her makeup. Her skin glowed even without the application of a blusher, but the skillful use of light and dark eye shadows and mascara emphasized the brilliant green of her eyes. Using a lip brush, she outlined her mouth with cinnamon, then filled in with a paler shade of the same hue.

Still wrapped in her bath towel, she stepped back from the mirror to study the effect of the makeup. Not bad, she told herself. Now, for the clothes.

She pulled on the most delicate undergarments she possessed, then a pale green half-slip with a deep lace flounce. She opened her closet to examine the clothes, pulling out dresses to hold against her body and then, dissatisfied, dropping them on the bed. She then moved to her aunt's closet, remembering a dress that was too small for Norma. If it fit, it would be perfect, modestly cut but clinging, in a gorgeous shade of emerald green with its own shawl of green and sapphire blue. Just the colors to make her red gold hair flame.

The dress fit perfectly, the high neck and long sleeves creating a demure quality until she turned around; her smooth, white back was exposed by an unexpectedly low neckline. The soft, semisheer fabric hugged her breasts and waist then flared into a flowing knee length skirt. Maybe just a little too dressy for a week night in Kennebunkport, but perfect for making a man lose sleep! And she did want Quinn to lose sleep!

She dug the matching shoes out of the shoebox that Norma had stored on her closet shelf and breathed a sigh of relief when they fit. Once more she viewed herself in the mirror. If she didn't look like a million dollars, she didn't look like a dime. She knew she was disregarding everything she had told herself about relationships, but if Quinn had cared enough to come after her, then maybe, just maybe, there was a future for them.

Grinning at herself in the mirror, she cocked a thumbs-up sign at her reflection, and ran downstairs to await Quinn's arrival.

The waiter poured the last of the wine into their glasses as Cara dug the last speck of lobster out of the last bit of claw. Quinn sat back, the upper half of his face in shadow, the light from the shaded candle on the table reflecting on his mouth and jaw.

"You really know how to attack a lobster, don't you? I've never seen one so thoroughly stripped before." His tone was complimentary, a hint of laughter underlying the words. "Or is it that your aunt doesn't feed you well enough?"

Cara put down her fork, lining it up beside the knife on her plate, a smug look on her face. "You really have to be a true down-easter to appreciate a lobster. It takes years to learn the technique." She sipped her wine as she accepted the dessert menu from the waiter. "The pies here are out of this world, especially the chiffons. I think I'll have the lemon. Although I love the pumpkin chiffon too, and the ginger is excellent. Oh-h-h, I can't make up my mind. What are you going to have?" She looked at Quinn, an appeal in her eyes.

"I'll have whatever you want," he answered her, a world of meaning in his words. His eyes locked onto hers, telling her exactly what it was that he did want. "How about ordering your two favorites and we'll share. That way you'll have everything."

"Well, maybe that might not be such a bad idea."

She answered him in the same silent language, telling him she was eager, but not yet so willing.

Quietly, Quinn gave their order to the waiter then turned to Cara. "I thought I'd be able to talk to you here, but it's not as easy as I thought it would be. Would you mind if I stopped in at the house when I take you home? There's so much I have to say . . ."

"I really don't know . . ." Cara made a show of reluctance. She felt in command at last, and for the moment she wanted Quinn to remain uncertain about her eventual surrender. "Let's wait until later to decide. Oh, here's the pie. Just wait until you taste this."

She managed to keep the conversation light until they were once again seated in his car. He turned to her, this time speaking in a more masterful way, and said, "We are going to talk now, aren't we, Cara? No more nonsense, right?"

"All right, Quinn, you can come in for a little while. I just don't know why you're so determined to talk, or what you want to say that brought you all the way up here."

"Well, now that you've waited this long, you can wait a few minutes longer." The smile on Quinn's face told Cara that he knew she was playing a game and that he was willing to go along with her. "I'd better pull into the driveway, it'll be easier to get to the walk."

Cara could sense that something momentous was going to happen this evening. Her breathing quickened with the hope that Quinn was finally ready to declare his love for her. It was the only thing that kept her from falling into his arms, the need to hear him say the words.

They had arrived at the cottage; he stopped the car and turned off the ignition. He climbed out, walked around the car and opened her door, being careful to touch only her hand when he reached in to help her out.

They were silent as they walked to the front door of the house. She groped in the narrow pouch bag she carried, feeling for the key; once she had found it, he took it from her, fitting it into the lock of the door to open it. He pushed at the door, allowing her to walk into the hallway before him.

"May I take your coat?" Cara felt like an explorer on the verge of a new adventure.

"Thank you." Quinn slowly removed his outer garment, then helped Cara with hers.

"Would you like some coffee?" She wasn't ready to start the play yet.

"No, thank you." Quinn turned his black eyes on her, a look of desire in them that made her bones melt.

"Let's . . . we'd . . ." Before she could say anything further, strong arms reached for her, enfolding her, enclosing her in their warmth. A hot mouth, burning, consuming, took possession of hers, forcing her lips apart. Her whole body seemed to bloom at his touch. She no longer wanted to hold him away from her; her desire now was to have him as close as possible. She was annoyed at the layers of clothing that separated the sensitive surfaces of their skin, afraid that they would not be able to surmount the obstacles that stood in the way of their closeness.

When he finally pulled his mouth from hers, they were both breathless. Still holding each other closely, they walked into the living room, finding a place on the couch.

"Oh, Cara, I've missed you more than I believed possible. Everything I ever thought or said or wrote about love proved to be wrong." He turned her face toward him, letting his fingertips trace the smooth line of her jaw, the straight length of her nose, the curve of her lips. His eyes followed his fingertip's movement.

She felt as though she were drowning in his look, feeling his love in that tender touch. "I never thought I'd see you again; I never thought I'd be in your arms again. Oh, Quinn! I died a thousand times when I left you." Once more the two lovers met in a kiss, now a gentle pledge.

"Cara darling, sweetheart, I love you. I've found out something about myself. I'm no longer afraid to say that I need you. Not just for a night, or a week, or a month, but for my whole life. I want you to be my wife, sharing my life, giving me children, who'll give us grandchildren and . . ."

The joy that Cara thought had been lost in Ithaca was back. She felt as though she would burst with excitement at Quinn's words. "Oh, Quinn . . . I can't believe this. What happened to change your mind?"

"I missed you. That's all, I missed you. You weren't there to see the funny side of the serious things occupying my days, you weren't there to laugh with or share with or love with. I found that the central part of my life had become empty . . . and no amount of work could fill that void. Wherever I went, I wanted to turn to you and say, look, Cara; see that, Cara; what do you think, Cara? But Cara wasn't there.

"I never tried to define love before, but if it includes all that, then I love you very, very much."

"Oh, I love you, I love you. I've loved you since the first time I met you, but you frightened me. I didn't realize what it was until we began to work together, but then I knew . . . right from the start. You're so backwards, what took you so long?" She laughed as she smoothed the hair back from his forehead.

"You knew the first time? I thought you had a memory lapse that night." An eyebrow quirked in question.

"I was ashamed. I didn't want you to think that I was so . . . . easy."

"I could never think that. What we had and have is very special to me. Tell me more." He held her closely, letting his love wrap around her.

"The night we met I was kind of unconscious, but conscious. I suppose you could say that my inhibitions were suspended for a few hours. So I didn't protest when an extraordinarily attractive man took me home with him."

"I thought you were high. I didn't realize you'd been in an accident, and then I got angry because you called me by your . . . you called me Donny. That made me furious, so I decided to seduce you when you were aware of what was happening. That's partly why you got the job at the magazine."

"Oh, Quinn, that was a terrible thing to do. I should be furious with you, but I'm glad you did it." She placed half a dozen quick kisses along his cheekbone and jawline. "Tell me more. This is better than reading a book!"

"Wench! Stop teasing." He pinched her leg to enforce his command. "Well, when you left New York, I decided that that was that. I wasn't going to change. I'd managed for such a long time without any commitments, I was not going to knuckle under now. But New York got to be very lonely. None of the women I dated were very interesting. No one excited me the way you did. No one *shared* with me the way you did. So after a month, I gave up. I knew that like it or not I was committed to you, but I wasn't sure that you'd still want me.

"I called your aunt. Oh, it was very hush, hush. In fact she made an appointment with me to call back because you were in the house that day and she couldn't speak freely. I felt as though I were in the middle of a spy movie. I think she loved making all the arrangements. I can't wait to meet her in person."

"Oh-h-h, that sly woman. She set this whole thing up, didn't she?"

"And am I glad she did. I might have chickened out if she hadn't, I was so sure you'd tell me to get lost. Anyway, that's what happened. So here I am."

"But what about the job? Was that part of the whole thing?"

"Well, in the ordinary course of events you would have been just a cog in the machine, as you thought when you came for the interview. But I couldn't let you get that far away from me. I had to set up a situation where we would be in constant contact." Cara laughed. "Stop that . . . or I'll . . ." he threatened.

"You'll what?" She couldn't stop beaming with happiness.

"I'll do this." Questing hands began to tickle her mercilessly. She jumped out of Quinn's embrace. "Oh no, you don't. You'll have to catch me first."

She dodged away from him, breathless with anticipation, and ran into the hall and up the stairs. She dashed into her bedroom and leapt onto her bed. When a disheveled Quinn followed her into the room, she was on her knees in the middle of the bed, her arms held wide. "You've caught me, my love. You've caught me."

Silhouette Desire 15-Day Trial Offer

A new romance series that explores contemporary relationships in exciting detail

Six Silhouette Desire romances, free for 15 days!
We'll send you six new Silhouette Desire romances
to look over for 15 days, absolutely free! If you decide
not to keep the books, return them and owe nothing.

Six books a month, free home delivery. If you like
Silhouette Desire romances as much as we think you
will, keep them and return your payment with the
invoice. Then we will send you six new books every
month to preview, just as soon as they are published.
You pay only for the books you decide to keep, and
you never pay postage and handling.

Silhouette Desire

Coming Next Month

Snow Spirit by Angel Milan

Joda Kerris' passions flared when she discovered that Egan, the man she had fallen in love with, was a lawyer hired to sue her and Keystone Mountain Ski Resort!

Meant To Be by Ann Major

Before she knew he was her boss, ravishing Leslie Grant abandoned herself to Boone Dexter for a single passionate night. Now could she convince him she loved him?

Fires Of Memory by Ashley Summers

Just when she thought he was safely out of her life, Adam Kendricks, real-estate tycoon, returned to San Francisco. This time Gia Flynn clung to one vow: to conquer him once and for all.

Silhouette Desire

Coming Next Month

Reckless Passion by Stephanie James

Dana Bancroft's stockbroker sense told her
that beneath Yale Ransom's well groomed
exterior there lurked a primal force . . .
anxiously waiting to be released.

Yesterday's Dreams by Rita Clay

He said his name was "Mr. Lawrence," but
Candra Bishop soon discovered the truth: he
was the stable boy she had adored in her youth
and now she was as much in his power as ever.

Promise Me Tomorrow by Nora Powers

Harris Lilton was a charmer, the kind of man
artist Jessie Hampton despised——yet couldn't
resist. She knew she couldn't trust him, but in
his arms she was heedless of all but desire.

Get 6 new Silhouette Special Editions every month for a 15-day FREE trial!

Free Home Delivery, Free Previews, Free Bonus Books.
Silhouette Special Editions are a new kind of romance novel. These are big, powerful stories that will capture your imagination. They're longer, with fully developed characters and intricate plots that will hold you spellbound from the first page to the very last.

Each month we will send you six exciting *new* Silhouette Special Editions, just as soon as they are published. If you enjoy them as much as we think you will, pay the invoice enclosed with your shipment. **They're delivered right to your door with never a charge for postage or handling, and there's no obligation to buy anything at any time.** To start receiving Silhouette Special Editions regularly, mail the coupon below today.

Silhouette Special Edition

Silhouette Special Editions ® is a registered trademark of Simon & Schuster